Atlanta Stories
Fables of the New South

G. M. Lupo

Lupo Digital Services, LLC
Atlanta, GA

Copyright © 2017 by G. M. Lupo

Fourth edition (paperback).

The cover photo is the skyline of Atlanta as seen from the Pryor Road overpass, facing North into town; taken 12 December 2017 around 16:32. Copyright © 2017, G. M. Lupo.

Library of Congress Number: TX 8-464-609

ISBN: 978-0-9848913-6-8. Published by Lupo Digital Services, LLC, Atlanta, Georgia (www.lupo.net). Printed in the United States of America.

Publication Notes

This work was originally published in its first paperback edition in July 2017, timed to coincide with the appearance of my play, *Another Mother*, in The Essential Theatre Festival, which features new work by Georgia playwrights. A second edition of the paperback was issued the following year, correcting a number of errors in the original. The third paperback and first hardcover edition represented a significant alteration of the original, incorporating major revisions of Mockingbird, Atomic Punk, and Phoenix, and significant updates of the remaining stories, and also included as its prologue a quote from Henry Grady's "The New South" speech, which inspired the title. The second hardcover and fourth paperback editions complete the synchronization with Reconstruction.

Acknowledgements

The author wishes to thank The Essential Theatre for their support and encouragement and everyone who bought a copy of the original work in whatever format purchased, and, in particular, those who offered reviews and commentary. Also, many thanks to Liz Dooley for her insightful comments and suggestions while editing this work in 2019.

Other Work by the Author

G. M. Lupo is the author of these works:

- Atlanta Stories: Reconstruction
- Words Words Words: Essays, Poetry, Stories
- Rebecca, Too
- The Long-Timer Chronicles

For new stories in development visit the author's blog Raised by Wolves at http://gmlupo.com.

G. M. Lupo can be found on the web at http://lupo.com.

To contact the author or to be added to the mailing list for future releases, send an email to author@gmlupo.com.

The New South is enamored of her new work. Her soul is stirred with the breath of a new life. The light of a grander day is falling fair on her face. She is thrilling with the consciousness of growing power and prosperity.

— Henry W. Grady, "The New South"
Delivered 22 December 1886

Mockingbird

Charlotte

Charlotte Sanger sits on a tree stump in the middle of the forest; she leans back, closes her eyes, and breathes in the cool air, listening to the sounds around her. The sun has been up for more than an hour, and Charlotte was here to witness all of it.

She likes the woods, away from everyone and everything; she sometimes sits for hours — thinking, sometimes singing, writing, or interacting with whatever woodland creature happens to cross her path. She's developed a talent for attracting animals, being very still and non-threatening, waiting for them to come to her. She's not very imposing, just a shade under five and a half feet tall, with long hair that reaches down her back to below her waist, which she often braids.

Charlotte's compulsion to repeat back words and phrases said to her, along with various facial tics and contortions, have earned her the nickname "Echo" at school. Her brothers and sisters started out calling her that around the house when she was little, but now many of her classmates also refer to her that way, albeit more derisively. The kids who've known her the longest, since nursery school or from her church and who've grown accustomed to her odd behavior, still call her Charlotte. When she was smaller some of the kids, for their amusement, would repeat back words to her, which only worsened her condition.

Her teachers are often annoyed by her disorder at first but come to realize she's very intelligent and studious, with an uncanny ability to focus on assignments, sometimes to the exclusion of all else. Ms. Warner, a math teacher, on her first day dealing with Charlotte, quickly became frustrated with her constant repetition.

"Are you mocking me, Charlotte?"

"Mocking, mocking, mock—" Charlotte replied. "No ma'am, Ms. Warner."

One of the other kids told Ms. Warner, "She can't help it. It's what she does."

"Perhaps you should come to the board and work out these equations," Ms. Warner said.

Charlotte got them all right, which impressed Ms. Warner. By the following class, Ms. Warner read up on echolalia and afterward, gave Charlotte a wide berth in class.

While Charlotte has trouble speaking, she has no trouble singing. In the choir at church, her contralto voice is considered one of the most beautiful among the members. Her older brother, Brian, who had been the choir director, realized that Charlotte could sing phrases she had trouble speaking and had been working with her to learn how to "sing" responses rather than say them. As a result, she often has a rhythmic cadence to her speech, almost like she's rapping, and sometimes she slips into singing words or phrases. Even still, she finds it hard to communicate and often shies away from people.

In the woods, however, she doesn't have to talk to anyone, and the animals she encounters don't judge how she communicates with them.

Brian had to leave town a few years ago due to an incident most town folk still don't talk about in the open, though Charlotte still hears whispers around her church and school. It involved Todd Williams, the pastor's son, and while her mother never said what it was, Charlotte knows Brian well enough and pretty much guessed at what had happened. She's heard Todd is still taking special classes with Pastor Williams, to learn how to be a better husband and father, which pretty much confirms everything Charlotte suspects. Brian is her favorite sibling, and has always been her chief protector, and Charlotte misses him terribly, but he told her before he left that she can come live with him in Atlanta when she graduates. That's now less than a year away.

She leans back on her hands and sings the lyrics to a new song she's been writing to the tune of a song she learned from the radio. Brian always added music to her lyrics and was teaching her to play guitar, another reason she misses him.

"When you see me
Please see through me
Find the person underneath
Hear the voice that calls to you
Give my spirit your relief."

She clears her head of all concerns and allows her mind to wander, allowing thoughts to drift in and out without letting them occupy too much of her consciousness. Nearby, she has her notebook, where she can write down any poems, stories, or new lyrics that come to her. While she's good at most subjects at school, her favorite is English, and her teachers have always encouraged her creative abilities. She channels everything she wants to say into her writing, routinely filling notebooks and journals with her words.

Her thoughts are interrupted by the sound of pine straw and twigs crunching. Something big is coming toward her, and Charlotte opens her eyes, expecting to see a deer, or a large dog. Instead a young man trudges into the clearing, looking like he has no idea where he is or how he got there.

He's at least six feet tall and well-built, wearing gym shorts and a varsity T-shirt, and jogging shoes. His dark hair is curly, and he's clean shaven. Charlotte recognizes him as Ned Branch, the captain of her high school football team, and the most popular guy in her school. He stands in the clearing a moment, as though trying to get his bearings, then turns toward Charlotte, and, seeing her, he smiles. She's at a loss for words.

"Oh, hey," he says. "I'm not lost anymore." He considers this. "Unless you're lost. Then I guess we both are."

Charlotte struggles to contain the impulse to repeat what he says.

"Was that you I heard singing?" Ned asks.

Charlotte nods with her lips pressed tightly together.

"You sound really good," he says. Approaching her, he goes on, "I'm Ned."

Charlotte opens her mouth to respond, but all that comes out is, "I'm Ned. N-Ned. Ned." She grimaces. Half-singing, "I'm Charlotte. Pleased to meet you, Ned."

"Hey, I know who you are. You're that girl they call Echo, right?"

"Echo, echo," Charlotte makes an effort to control herself. "Some people call me that."

"You don't like it, do you?"

She shakes her head.

"Then I won't call you that, okay? Why are you out here in the woods?"

Charlotte looks away from him. In a mixture of speech and song, she says, "I like it here. It's quiet. No one's around."

"Nobody but me, right?"

"Why are you here?"

Ned shrugs and leans against a tree. "Coach said it might be good to go running in the woods. Said it heightens our awareness or something like that. Of course, I forgot my Walkman with all my tunes on it."

"On it, on it. It's better to keep your ears open. You can hear the forest sounds around you. The birds. The animals moving around."

He nods. "Yeah, that's a good idea. I wouldn't want something sneaking up on me." He strolls around the clearing. "What do you do out here all by yourself."

"Sing, write, think. Sometimes I just listen."

"Yeah, there is a lot of noise out here," he says.

"It's the birds, mostly. Sometimes squirrels. Sometimes other things. I thought you might be a deer at first."

"That'd be something, wouldn't it? What was the song you were singing?"

"Singing, singing," she says. "Just something I'm working on."

"You wrote that?"

"The words. I don't write music yet."

"Can I hear it?" he says. "I mean, I kind of already have, but can I hear more?"

Charlotte lowers her head. "If you want."

"Sure." Ned crouches down nearby.

Charlotte sings a few verses of her song, using the music from before. When she finishes, Ned claps. "You're great. Have any others?"

Charlotte sings one she wrote with Brian.

"You ask, who am I? Can I be
The me you'll never see?
You see my face,
You hear me speak,
And still we're miles apart.
I just want you to take my hand
and touch my soul
and let me know your heart.
Still it seems, I'll always be
The me you'll never see."

"You should get a recording contract," Ned says. "You've got a great voice."

"Thanks."

Ned rises and looks around. "You must know your way around out here."

Charlotte nods.

"Think you could show me?" he says. "I was running around for nearly an hour before I heard you."

"Sure. I can do that." She gathers her things and puts them in her bag and rises. "Want to see the lake?"

"There's a lake? Sure."

Charlotte takes the lead, guiding Ned along a trail. As they move along, she moves her head left and right slowly, as though she's looking for something.

"What are you doing?" Ned asks.

"Listening."

A short way on, she stops and holds up her hand. She focuses on something to her right, then points. Ned looks, but doesn't see anything at first. Suddenly, a deer appears, followed by two fawns. They wander around, nibbling on leaves and grass, before disappearing back into the woods.

"That was cool," he said. "I guess you do need to pay attention out here."

They continue on until they arrive at the lake. Several ducks are on the shore, but as Charlotte and Ned approach, they start quacking and get into the water, swimming quickly toward the middle.

Charlotte and Ned sit on some rocks.

"This is nice," he says. "I see why you like it out here."

"You've never been out here before?"

"No. I always played in the park downtown when I was a kid. Other than that, I've always been busy with practice and stuff. Plus, I have to study a lot. I'm not doing all that great. Coach says if I can maintain my grades, I could get a scholarship to UGA."

"You're really good," Charlotte says. "I thought we were going to lose that game last week, but you threw that pass and brought us back."

"Oh, I'm good. Coach says I'm the best QB he's worked with but says football alone isn't going to get me very far, not even in Georgia."

"Georgia, Georgia," Charlotte repeats.

"Why do you do that?" Ned asks. "I mean is there some medical explanation?"

"Maybe. I've just always done it. Ever since I was little. A counselor in middle school told me it was a learning disorder, but I don't have trouble learning, just talking."

"People at school tease you, right?"

"Some do."

"Tell you what. Next time kids at school start bothering you, let me know. I'll stop 'em."

Charlotte laughs. "Okay."

They talk for more than an hour about school and favorite teachers and classes, then Charlotte leads Ned back to where he says he parked.

"Look me up on Monday," he tells her. "Maybe you can help me with my homework."

"What will your girlfriend say?"

"Lindsay? She could use some help, too. Maybe you can teach us both something."

When Charlotte arrives at school the following Monday, she finds Ned waiting for her with his girlfriend Lindsay Maddox, the head cheerleader. Ned greets her warmly, but Lindsay doesn't seem so pleased.

"Echo? She's the one you say can tutor me?"

"Don't call her that," Ned says. "It's not nice."

Lindsay turns to Charlotte. "How good are you at Algebra?"

"Algebra, algebra," Charlotte repeats. "I passed it in tenth grade. You're still taking it?"

"I need it to graduate," Lindsay says.

"Graduate, graduate," Charlotte replies. She forces herself to be silent.

"How did you do, Charlotte?" Ned says.

Half singing, she replies, "I'm good at math. I got an A."

"See? She's a star student."

"Well, okay," Lindsay says. "I'll give her a try. I suppose you're going to repeat everything I say."

"Say, say, say," Charlotte replies. "I can't really help it."

They get together after school at Lindsay's home. Charlotte starts out slowly going over the assignments but begins to realize she doesn't need to take her time, since Lindsay seems to pick up the material quickly. After a few days, Lindsay demonstrates a proficiency Charlotte had not expected.

"Lindsay, you can do this stuff," Charlotte says. "You picked it up really quick."

"It's easier than I thought it would be," she says. "The way you explain it makes more sense than hearing the teachers talk about it."

"Maybe you're smarter than you let on," Charlotte says.

"I'm not expected to be smart," Lindsay says. "Nobody wants a smart cheerleader. I'm expected to smile, and be pretty, and marry the right man, and spend my life supporting him. I'm not allowed to be sad, or tired, or knowledgeable. I'm just supposed to make somebody else feel happy and believe in himself."

"You can be all those things with me, if you want," Charlotte says. "I won't say anything."

Lindsay takes Charlotte's hand. "Thank you for saying that. I'm sorry if I ever said or did anything to upset you."

"Mostly you just ignored me," Charlotte says.

"I won't do that again, okay?"

"Thanks," Charlotte says.

"I noticed something," Lindsay says. "When you relax, you don't have so much trouble talking."

"I noticed that, too," Charlotte says.

They spend their afternoons studying, after Lindsay's finished with practice, and Lindsay masters most of the subjects they cover. She's impressed with Charlotte's knowledge and patience and isn't bothered by the occasional times Charlotte's condition intrudes on their conversation. Charlotte is pleased to find Lindsay's much more friendly and open than she imagined she'd be. The two quickly become friends.

As a consequence of becoming friends with the head cheerleader, Charlotte suddenly finds that people who once mercilessly teased her for her condition now rarely mention it and other girls close to Lindsay seek her out for advice on lessons, or to be in study groups. Several express an interest in making her over, and a few of Ned's teammates on the football team admit they find Charlotte "kind of cute". Charlotte takes it in stride, never allowing herself to forget how she was treated before gaining the attention of someone popular. Still, she finds the attention a welcome relief from the taunts she once endured.

One person who shows a lot of interest in Charlotte is Stanley Clemons, a wide receiver on the football team. As children, he and Charlotte attended the same church, but after his parents divorced and his mother remarried, his family switched denominations. He's a second-string player, usually a bench warmer, with plans to attend Abraham Baldwin Agricultural College in Tifton after he graduates high school. His father has already promised him some acreage on his property once Stanley finishes college, with an eye toward Stanley taking over the farm someday.

Since Charlotte has become good friends with Lindsay and Stanley plays on the team with Ned, Lindsay proposes they start going on double dates to the movies or on other excursions. This meets with Ned's approval, but after a few outings, Charlotte and

Stanley find they have little in common and don't talk much when they're out. Stanley mostly talks about farming and his plans for agricultural college, while Charlotte prefers talking about music and writing. Stanley doesn't have much of a voice and confesses that he often just hums the lyrics to hymns in church. For the most part, they're very awkward together, and on double dates, Charlotte spends most of her time talking to Lindsay, while Stanley relegates himself to listening to Ned brag about the latest successful play he called during their most recent game. After about a month, both Charlotte and Stanley start making excuses whenever Lindsay or Ned proposes another outing.

As the Homecoming game approaches nominations go out for the queen and her court, and someone nominates Charlotte. No one expects her to win, since it's a forgone conclusion that the king and queen will be Ned and Lindsay, but Charlotte does receive enough votes to make the top five, putting her on the field when the winner is announced. Since only the faculty adviser tallies the votes, there's sufficient uncertainty to warrant a good deal of nervousness on her part.

She's also stressed over the fact that she doesn't have a gown to wear for the ceremony. Lindsay offers to help her pick one out, but Charlotte's mother informs her that she's not going to pay a fortune for a new dress Charlotte will only wear once. This prompts a call to Brian, who puts Charlotte in touch with a seamstress he used for choir robes. Lindsay gives Charlotte the dress she wore at last year's Homecoming, and Charlotte has it modified to fit her with a few extra flourishes to make it look like less of a hand-me-down.

The morning of the game, Mrs. Townsend, the faculty adviser, announces the vote tally, without saying who'll be Homecoming Queen. "This was the closest vote we've ever had as long as I've been here. This year's queen will be elected by a single vote."

This causes a lot of buzz throughout the school, since it casts doubt on everyone's belief that Lindsay will be the Queen. For her part, Charlotte spends most of the day hoping no one's planning on pouring blood all over her. That night at the game, Ned leads the team to a 24-12 lead by halftime, and once the clock runs out, a red carpet is rolled out to form the runway, and the band takes its place to either side. The five candidates for queen come forward and line up. Most of the girls are escorted by their fathers, but

Charlotte asked her brother Dexter to be her escort, since their father is dead, and Brian still can't show his face in town.

The principal is handed the envelope and slides out the card, considering it for a few seconds, before saying, "We're pleased to announce this year's Homecoming Queen — Charlotte Sanger!"

Lindsay is the first person to hug Charlotte as the crowd in the stadium erupts in deafening cheers. Lindsay whispers to Charlotte, who seems frozen in place, "You need to step forward and let them give you your sash and crown."

Charlotte nods and complies. The principal puts the sash on her and places the crown on her head. As he does, reality finally catches up to her and tears start rolling down her cheeks. She holds up her bouquet, and waves to the crowd before being congratulated by the rest of the court, some hugging her. The team goes on to win the game by 42-26. At the dance, Charlotte dances the first dance with Ned, who was voted King, and poses for pictures with him.

Charlotte later learns she was the candidate who many of the less popular students voted for in opposition to Lindsay who usually wins everything. Still, she's curious about the one vote that made the difference.

"I wonder who it was who put me over the top?" Charlotte says.

"I think I did," Lindsay says. "I voted for you."

"Why?' Charlotte asks. "Didn't you want to be Homecoming queen? Everybody thought you would be."

"I didn't know how close the vote would be," Lindsay says, "but I'm not sorry how it turned out. Ten years from now, it wouldn't have meant anything to me. But knowing you got it will mean a lot more."

Charlotte gives her a long hug. "Thank you."

About a month before prom, Ned and Lindsay have a big fight and break up.

Their disagreement centers around college versus marriage, and while neither of them consider skipping college, given Ned's prospects for a lucrative scholarship, Lindsay thinks they should be married before they go, while Ned wants them to wait, at least until they see how things work out at school. The argument escalates to the point that Lindsay refuses to attend prom with Ned unless he comes to his senses, and he digs in his heels, threatening to find another date.

Being friendly with them both, Charlotte finds herself caught between the two extremes. Ned tells her she's lucky she'll be attending the prom with Stanley, and when Charlotte informs him Stanley's taking someone else and she isn't planning on attending, this prompts Ned to ask her to be his date. Lindsay's reaction isn't what Charlotte expects.

"I think you should go," she tells Charlotte. "If Ned's not going with me, I'd rather it be someone else I like."

"Aren't you going?" Charlotte asks her.

"No, I'll be out of town that night," Lindsay says. "That's what I'm telling everyone."

"Will you really be out of town?"

"I'll probably go to Dublin and watch a movie, so yes," Lindsay says.

Agreeing to be Ned's date causes several problems for Charlotte. Since meeting him in the woods that day, Charlotte has developed a crush on him, but she can't decide if she truly loves him or if she loves all he represents, the attention, the show of respect the students give him, the envy the other girls have of Lindsay when she's with Ned. Charlotte's sensible enough to realize he hasn't suddenly fallen head over heels in love with her, and that his intentions to take her to the prom are just to make his girlfriend jealous. Still, the thought of walking into her senior prom on the arm of the captain of the football team is very appealing to Charlotte, who's painfully aware that people describe her as "mousy" and "weird".

Just after Homecoming, Charlotte took an afternoon job at a restaurant near her home to save up some money to help her get to Atlanta when she graduates. As prom approaches, she checks her finances and decides she has enough to afford a nice dress without seriously depleting her nest egg. Lindsay goes with her to a dress shop in Dublin, where they decide on an emerald green ballgown that perfectly complements Charlotte's strawberry blonde hair and hazel eyes. She has just enough left over to afford a nice pair of shoes to go with the dress.

When Ned picks up Charlotte the night of the prom, he stares at her for a long moment, before saying, "Wow. You look great."

"Great, great," she repeats. "Thanks."

He presents her with an orchid, which she pins on her left shoulder and they hop into his car and head to the country club where the dance is being held.

Their school district had been under fire until four years ago for having separate proms for blacks and whites, which had been rectified by holding the first integrated prom around the time Charlotte was in ninth grade. Now, many of the students wonder why it had been such a big deal, as the subsequent events have gone off without a hitch, and the school saves a lot of money by not having to rent two spaces. There are still quite a few parents who won't allow their sons and daughters to attend the integrated affair.

At the dance, Charlotte has her photo taken with Ned, and they dance a bit, but mostly hang out at their table with several other football players and their dates. Ned talks a bit about Lindsay, wondering where she went and what she's doing tonight. Charlotte doesn't mention that Lindsay said she'd be watching a movie in Dublin, allowing Ned to believe Lindsay's actually in some exotic location, like Macon or Savannah.

Charlotte has noticed on more than one occasion that when Ned's not talking about Lindsay, he tends to talk a lot about his own accomplishments. Most of his stories revolve around some play he made to save a game, or some compliment the Coach gave him, or what he plans to do once he goes to UGA. She's often observed Lindsay with him, patiently listening to what he's saying, not displaying how she feels about it, though Charlotte did note on those occasions when she and Stanley double-dated with Ned and Lindsay, Lindsay seemed happy to have someone with whom she could talk while Stanley listened to Ned's stories.

As the prom starts to wind down, several students mention a party that's happening at a private home outside of town, where there might be a keg. Ned seems interested, but Charlotte tells him she'd rather not go someplace where there's alcohol. Neither of them is ready to head home, so Ned proposes they stop by his sister's apartment, which he's been watching while she's away on vacation, where they can hang out and talk. Once there, Charlotte kicks off her shoes, sits on the couch, and puts her feet up on an ottoman, while Ned removes his tuxedo jacket and tie and unbuttons the first two buttons on his shirt. He joins her on the couch.

"Sing something for me," he says.

"What do you want to hear?" she asks.

"Have anything new?" he says. "It doesn't' matter. I love hearing you sing."

She sings a new song she's been writing about leaving home, then follows it up with an older number about a boyfriend and girlfriend trying to communicate. Without either noticing, they move closer together as she sings. She finishes singing and looks at Ned, whose eyes are glued on her. He leans toward her and kisses her lightly on the lips. She stares into his eyes and they kiss again for several seconds.

"We don't have to go any further if you don't want," he says.

"I want to," she says.

"Are you sure?"

"Sure, sure, sure," she repeats. Instead of trying to speak, she just kisses him again.

A couple of hours later, they're lying together in bed, Ned's arm around Charlotte and her head resting on his shoulder.

"It was your first time, right?" Ned says.

"It was."

"Are you okay?" he says.

"I'm great," she says.

"You know, me and Lindsay are probably going to get back together," he says.

"I know," she says. "That's okay. I just always wondered what this would be like."

"Was it what you expected?"

"I'm not sure," she says. "It was different."

"I'll take different," he says. "When does your mom get off work?"

"Work, work. She's covering the night shift and won't be back until morning."

"I guess I should get you back home," he says.

"Probably."

A while later, Charlotte arrives home feeling happier than she's ever been. Her evening with Ned has satisfied any feelings she's had for him, which relieves her, since she's certain he'll end up going back to Lindsay once they've both had time to reevaluate things. Charlotte has decided than unless Lindsay asks her directly, she won't even say anything about the encounter with Ned.

As expected, Lindsay and Ned reconcile, and Lindsay agrees not to insist on them being married before arriving at UGA given the other challenges they'll face there, and Ned agrees to consider getting married once they've settled in, maybe in a year. They begin plotting their life together once high school is over. Charlotte and Lindsay go on with their friendship as though nothing happened.

One month later, a few days after graduation, Charlotte misses her period. Trying to keep her wits about her, she takes a trip to a pharmacy in Dublin, where she picks up an early pregnancy test which she uses once she's home. It confirms what she already knows.

After Charlotte tells Ned she's pregnant, he turns to the person he always relies on for advice outside his family: Harold Ricketts, the football coach. Coach Ricketts has already been told by Ned's father to make sure Ned reaches the "right conclusion for him" and wastes no time setting Ned straight on what his priorities should be.

"You have talent, son, potential," Coach says. "You don't need to waste it in rural Georgia married to some freak."

"She's not a freak. She's real smart. She's got talent, too."

"Singing in church?" Ricketts says. "That's going to matter a lot when you're working overtime at Bickering Textiles, or the agricultural plant to pay for a wife and kids. Think of all you're throwing away, son."

Ned doesn't answer.

"Do you even love this girl?" Ricketts goes on.

"I don't know," Ned says. "I like her a lot."

"That's just fine and dandy," Coach Ricketts says. "Hey, Ned, why'd you throw away your chance at college and maybe even the NFL? Well, I really liked this girl. How do you even know you're the father?"

"She was a virgin when we did it," Ned says.

"How do you know?"

"You know, the way you tell," Ned says.

"What's the chance she'll keep the kid?" Ricketts says.

"Abortion?"

"Of course not," Ricketts says. "Adoption."

"I doubt it," Ned says. "She's always talking about how close her family is. Doesn't seem like something she'd consider."

"Wasn't she going out with Stanley?" Ricketts says.

"It wasn't more than a few times. I don't think they like each other all that much."

"Then there's your ticket out," Coach says. "Stanley doesn't have any kind of a future. He's going to agricultural college next year. Nobody's recruiting him."

"But it's not right," Ned says. "I'm not blaming this on Stanley."

"What's not right is you throwing away your chance at the big time," Ricketts says. "You don't even have to do anything. Just let me put the word in a few ears. That's all it'll take."

While Ned doesn't totally agree with Coach Ricketts's approach, he definitely wants to attend UGA and agrees to not say anything to indicate he's the responsible party. In a few days, rumors are circulating that Stanley is the father of a child Charlotte's carrying. Stanley's family insists that if it's true, Stanley must marry Charlotte. Coach Ricketts offers his assistance in sorting out the situation and Stanley's parents ask him to talk to their son.

"I don't even like Charlotte that much," Stanley says. "I mean, she's nice, but we didn't really hit it off. I don't know why people think I have anything to do with this."

"It just takes that one time, son," Ricketts says. "That's why it pays to be responsible."

"I ain't even been out with Charlotte for months," Stanley says. "I saw her at the prom, but we hardly talked. My family's telling me I might have to marry her."

"Is that such a bad thing? Way I hear it, she's a sweet little girl."

"We don't have anything in common."

"That's the thing about relationships, son," Coach Ricketts says. "Once you get in one, you grow closer."

"Ain't you been divorced? Like twice?"

"We're not here to talk about me, son," Ricketts says. "You need to take responsibility for your actions. It's the manly thing to do."

"I take responsibility when I'm responsible. I'm not involved with this."

After talking to Stanley, Ricketts offers his opinion to Stanley's parents that Stanley isn't being totally forthcoming with his responses. This convinces them Stanley is lying about being involved and they insist he "do right by Charlotte." The Coach offers to meet with Amelia Sanger on their behalf. She's not so easy to convince.

"Charlotte told me the whole story," Amelia says.

"You sure you can trust that?" he says. "Way I hear it, she's been following Ned around for months, pining over him."

"Over him, over him, over," Charlotte repeats. "It's not true."

"I trust her a lot more than I trust you, Ricketts. Coming in here wanting to save your golden boy so he can play for UGA. My daughter's a decent, God-fearing girl. She don't lie to me."

Ricketts leans toward Charlotte. "Ned ain't going to marry you girl."

"Girl, girl," she repeats. She throws her hand over her mouth, shakes her head, then says, "I don't want to marry Ned. I just want him to say what he did."

"That's not going to happen either," Ricketts tells her. "Ned's on his way to Athens to get ready for school."

"Athens ain't that far away," Amelia says. "I could drive it in an afternoon. I'll drag his sorry ass back here and see what he has to say about all this."

"I wouldn't go doing that if I was you," Coach says. "Word's already gotten out about this. How do you enjoy singing in that choir now? Oh, that's right. They kicked you out didn't they."

"Mama?" Charlotte says. Amelia holds up her hand.

"I figured you were the lowdown dog who started those rumors," Amelia says. "You or that family of Ned's."

"I take care of my own," Coach says. "You'd be well advised to do the same."

After Amelia leaves for work, Charlotte rides her bike to the Piggly Wiggly, where Stanley works as a stocker and bagger. Seeing her, he takes a break and they go around to the side of the store to talk.

"I don't want to marry you, Stanley," Charlotte says. "No offense, but I just don't want to be your wife."

"I don't want to marry you either," Stanley says. "No offense. You're a nice enough girl and all, but I don't want to spend the rest of my life with you."

"Then why are you doing this?" Charlotte asks.

"My parents are making me," he says. "They won't believe me when I tell them I'm not involved."

"Involved, involved, involved," Charlotte repeats. She shakes her head violently. "You know it's that coach who started the rumors."

"Yeah, that's what I figured," Stanley says. "I don't like this anymore than you do, Charlotte. But it's looking like I don't have much choice. My parents won't believe me and insist I need to do something about this."

"About this, about this. Thanks for all your help, Stanley," she says and walks away.

Charlotte continues to worry what will happen and a few days later, takes refuge in the one place she's most happy, the forest. She heads toward the lake, where she's surprised to find Ned sitting on a rock.

"Ned, what are you doing here?"

"Hey, Charlotte. I was hoping I'd get to see you," Ned says.

"They said you were in Athens."

"I'm supposed to be," he says. "They don't know I'm here."

"Here, here, here," she stops herself. "Why are you here?"

"I wanted to see you — to say I'm sorry for everything," he tells her.

"Sorry, sorry, sorry? You think that's going to make up for anything?"

"I hope it makes up for something," he says.

"They're trying to get me to marry Stanley," she says.

"I know. Coach Ricketts says it's for the best."

"Coach, coach, coach says," Charlotte spits out. "Did you ever think about how I feel about it?"

"I'm just some dumb football player, Charlotte. I don't have anything else. I like you. I like you a lot. But it's nothing to start a life on."

"With Lindsay maybe," Charlotte says.

"Maybe," he says.

"She won't return my calls," she tells him.

"Lindsay's in Athens," Ned says. "She doesn't know I'm here, either."

"Then you better get back to her," Charlotte says.

"Look, this whole thing has all gone too far," Ned says. "It's out of my hands. I wish I could do something, but I can't."

"Then I guess there's nothing else to say," Charlotte says, looking away from him. "You should go. You've got a long drive ahead of you."

"I wish we didn't have to leave it like this," Ned says.

"Like this, like this. That's not my choice."

When Charlotte gets back to her house, she's surprised to find Coach Ricketts there with her mother.

"What's he doing here?" Charlotte asks.

Coach Ricketts looks at Amelia. "I believe you have something to say, here, Mrs. Sanger."

Amelia motions for Charlotte to sit on the couch.

"I just got off the phone with Stanley's mother," Amelia says. "Tomorrow afternoon, he's coming by to ask you to marry him."

"Mama, no."

Amelia holds up her hand. "I don't want to hear your objections." Emphatically, she continues, "You know what I expect you to do. What we talked about."

Charlotte lowers her head. "Yes, Mama."

Amelia gives Charlotte a long, tight hug then rises. "I know you'll do the right thing. Now I need to get to work."

"I'll walk out with you," Coach Ricketts says. Turning to Charlotte, he says, "This is the right solution for all concerned."

He steps out to the porch. Amelia pauses and says to Charlotte with a slight crack in her voice, "Take care of yourself, my sweet girl."

She exits.

Charlotte says after her, "Goodbye, Mama."

Once she hears both cars leave the driveway, Charlotte goes to the kitchen and calls Brian.

Brian

Brian Sanger is in the Starbucks at 1776 Peachtree Street, halfway through a venti, black, dark-roast, Ethiopian coffee, and an almond scone, looking over a piece of music he's composing. He typically prefers Caribou to Starbucks, but has yet to replace his car since it was totaled in an accident late last year, and he doesn't live close enough to the Caribou at Ansley to pop in whenever he feels like it, plus, he's hooked on the Blue Note blend his friend, Claire Belmonte, convinced him to try a week or so before. He can easily walk from his apartment to the Starbucks on Peachtree, so he stops in every few days to stock up on coffee, try out whatever dark roast they've brewed up that day, and work on his music. Certain days, Claire joins him if she's worked a club nearby.

When Brian arrived in Atlanta, the Braves were in the middle of their "worst to first" season and the city had won the privilege of hosting the Olympics the previous year. While he never considered himself much of a sports fan, aside from high school football games he had to attend with the band, he found himself getting caught up in the fervor surrounding the team, but usually couldn't afford to attend games, instead watching them when they were on the television at bars he inhabited.

In addition to becoming a baseball fan, Brian has spent much of his first years in town familiarizing himself with the gay scene in Atlanta and it was here he met Claire, who had gone to work as a bartender at his favorite hangout as soon as she turned twenty-one in '94. He recognized her from the Unitarian Universalist Congregation he's been attending. She explained that she'd been working as a waitress in restaurants and bars while studying sound engineering in junior college and had grown tired of dealing with the patrons. She told Brian that the manager of the gay club hired her to tend bar there despite her lack of experience for the same reason she applied for the job. The men don't hit on her. Plus, the older men treat her like a daughter and leave better tips. The manager sometimes lets her run the sound board during the week when one of the regular deejays is gone.

Almost as if on cue, Claire enters and looks around. Spotting Brian, she gives a quick nod, then stops at his table. She's very close to his own height of six feet three inches, with long dark hair she usually pulls back, especially if she's working. From the moment they first met, Brian was struck by her expressive brown eyes and she greets him with a charming smile that she only displays to those she knows well. To everyone else, she's an ice princess. Since arriving in Atlanta, she's been taking T'ai Chi classes to improve her fitness and learn to defend herself.

"What are you having?" Claire asks.

"Today's dark roast."

She seems less than enthused and dumps her bag onto the seat beside Brian and goes to check out the pastry counter.

Claire has a non-distinct "Atlanta" accent, which she's worked hard to cultivate since she arrived here as a teen, but when she and Brian are together, she often ditches it in favor of her original Middle Georgia vernacular. She grew up a little more than fifty miles west of where Brian had been raised, far enough away for it to take coming to Atlanta for them to meet. She has quite a complicated past, which included physical and emotional abuse, and she's been gradually revealing details to Brian as he gains her trust. He knows she came from a deeply religious family and he's always believed that lessened the options for a young woman coming of age in rural Georgia, with many feeling pressure to marry and start families early. Her difficulty in trusting people tells him much of the story.

Learning more about what Claire has experienced deepens his conviction to bring his sister Charlotte to Atlanta when she finishes high school. Their brother and sisters all married straight out of high school and started families, though all were good candidates for higher learning, and Charlotte has always expressed a desire to continue her education and develop her talent for music. Brian feels she'd have a better shot at that in Atlanta.

Brian is the oldest sibling in his family of two sons and three daughters, raised mostly by their mother after his father died in an accident at the agricultural plant where he'd worked most of his adult life. Brian sang in the choir at his church and was in the brass section in his high school marching band. He's also accomplished on the piano and organ and plays guitar. When she was a toddler, Charlotte would sit nearby while he was practicing, enrapt by the music. His background in music and his involvement in their church made it almost inevitable that he'd be approached about taking over the choir when the previous director retired. It was in his role as choir director where Brian gained the attention of Todd, the son of their pastor, Kenneth Williams.

Todd was the first guy from outside Brian's peer group who had shown any interest in him and seemed more sophisticated than most of Brian's friends with whom he'd graduated. Brian didn't know how to interpret the signals Todd was sending him, given that Todd was in his mid-twenties, married, and had two little girls at home. Todd had been very persistent, however, and finally coaxed Brian into a clandestine relationship, which was mostly carried out at Todd's house on days when his wife was out running errands or attending church functions. Brian suggested that it might not be the best idea to have their encounters at Todd's home, but Todd insisted they'd have complete privacy.

This proved to be wrong when Todd's wife showed up unexpectedly, after her women's devotional group ended early, having found the book of Revelation too cryptic to be digested in a two-hour lunchtime conversation. After most of the screaming and yelling had devolved into tears and apologies (during which time Brian hastily pulled on his clothes) he bowed politely to the couple and excused himself with, "I'll just be on my way now."

Two hours later, the call came from Pastor Williams. By then, Brian had already written his letter resigning as choir director, packed his bags, and loaded up his car, since he knew it was probably best not to stick around. He gave his mother a somewhat expanded explanation about what had happened after she'd already heard an abbreviated version from the pastor, and left a letter for Charlotte, letting her know he'd stay in touch, and renewing his promise to bring her to Atlanta when she graduated. Once his meeting with the pastor was concluded, he hit I-16 west toward Macon, and from there, took I-75 north to Atlanta.

"Do you want to check out Dad's Garage?" Brian says when Claire rejoins him at the table. She's armed with a cinnamon bun and a cappuccino to which she immediately adds four or five packets of sugar.

"I don't have a car and neither do you," Claire replies. "Why would we go to a garage?"

"No, they're this new theater group. I hear they do improvisation. Like on that show *Whose Line is It Anyway?*"

"I don't watch television," she says. "I suppose we could give it a try. As long as we can get there on MARTA."

"They're in Little Five Points."

"Sure, why not?"

"I want to see how they use music in their shows," he says.

"You think they'll hire you?"

"It's a possibility. The theater scene around Atlanta is improving. They're bound to need musicians. Especially with the Olympics coming."

"Decatur's the place for music," she says. "I caught the open mic night at the Attic last Monday. You should do that some week."

"Is it hard to get a spot?"

"No. I think you just call 'em up and see if there's room. They give a cash prize."

"It's a competition? Think I have a chance?"

"I've heard you sing. Yeah. You could do well."

"Hey, about that other group, the Jaycees?" he says.

"What about them?" she says.

"You want to check 'em out?" he asks.

"I'm not going to pretend to be your girlfriend," she says.

"Have I ever asked you that?" he says. "I just don't like walking in places by myself. We wouldn't have to join. I just want to see what they're all about."

"They had the Jaycees in Perry once," Claire says. "I heard people talk about them when I was growing up."

"Yeah, they had them where I lived too, but I think they're more business oriented here," he says.

"Don't they do the Empty Stocking Fund?"

"I think so," he says.

"I wouldn't mind getting involved with that," she says. "A woman I worked with at a restaurant a few years ago said they were a big help one Christmas when she was between jobs and on welfare."

"Let's check them out, then," he says.

"Oh, okay," she says. "At least we'll have an active social calendar. Eddie's first, though. You need to be on stage."

Brian follows Claire's suggestion and starts competing in open mic nights around Atlanta. One of his frequent competitors is a woman known in the clubs as "Banjo Girl" because her songs are a mixture of Bluegrass, Country, and Jazz, and she always accompanies herself on the banjo. Brian learns that her name is Deanna Savage, and she's a married mother of three from Norcross. Sometimes, when she knows she's early in the lineup, her husband Manny, who's also a performer, brings their young children, Derek, Gloria, and Prudence to hear their mother perform.

Once he gets to know them, Brian looks forward to bringing Charlotte to Atlanta and introducing her to the Savages. The couple met when they were students at Perimeter College in the 80s and married shortly after graduation. Musicians, singers, and music lovers, they named their three children after favorite songs and groups, Derek, the oldest, after Derek and the Dominos, and Prudence, their youngest, after the Beatles song. Their middle daughter, Gloria, was named after the Van Morrison song, though Manny knew it via the Jimi Hendrix cover, whereas Deanna was more familiar with the Patti Smith version.

Since they started dating and playing music together, Deanna and Manny have made themselves fixtures in the Atlanta music scene, and after they married, their home in Norcross quickly became a hub for food, fellowship, and music. They wasted no time instilling their children with a love for music, song, and storytelling, and hold monthly jams on weekends at their home. Brian and Claire are always invited, and Claire gains valuable experience helping out with the soundboard for shows.

Whenever Brian and Claire join them, either Manny or Deanna will pick them up at Doraville MARTA station, and they often end up spending the night, along with others, who sleep on any available floor space indoors or on the enclosed back porch. The music often goes on until the wee small hours, since the Savages encouraged fellow musicians to move in next door, and often they join in the shows. The following morning, Manny and Deanna cook up a massive breakfast for whoever's still hanging around.

Brian finally convinces Claire to go to the monthly meeting of the Atlanta Jaycees, which is held the first Thursday of the month in Buckhead. As Claire and Brian are walking toward the hotel entrance, dressed in business attire, an older woman, wearing a floral print dress and red sweater, in work shoes with white socks, and carrying a duffle bag approaches them from behind.

She calls out to Claire: "Christine".

They both turn, and Claire seems startled. Brian just barely hears her say, "Mama?"

Brian looks between them. "This is your mother?"

Claire looks at him then pulls herself together. Utilizing her Atlanta accent, she says, "No, Brian. I've never seen this woman before in my life. Let's go."

They start to walk, Brian looking back over his shoulder at the woman.

"Christine, please. I need your help."

Brian pauses, but Claire keeps walking and says over her shoulder, "I'm sorry. You've mistaken me for someone else. My name is Claire Belmonte."

Brian starts to follow but before they go very far, the woman calls out, "Christine, I left your father."

Claire stops and closes her eyes, then says in a measured voice, "Brian, would you mind waiting for me inside?"

"No problem," he says, but his instincts tell him not to leave them alone. Instead, he ducks behind a column a few feet away to observe.

Claire approaches the woman, seething. "Don't you ever — ever! — call that man my father. You and I both know he isn't and never was."

"He may not be your father, but I'm your mother."

"How can that be? I know for a fact your only daughter's dead." The woman looks down.

"Yeah, that's right," Claire continues. "I've been down there." She practically spits out the words, "I left flowers on her grave."

"I'm sorry about all that."

"It's a little too late for sorry," Claire says. "What do you want, and make it fast, I've got things to do."

"I got nowhere to go. Spent all my money coming here. I need help," the woman says.

"Call Alvin," Claire says.

"Alvin hasn't talked to me in years. I'm not welcome in his house anymore."

"Well, that's for a good reason," Claire says.

"You got to help me."

"I seem to recall a time I asked you the same thing, and you turned your back on me."

"You know what he's capable of, Christine. I can't let him find me."

"Yeah? You knew what he was capable of all those years you condemned me to live under his roof, when all you had to do was be honest and it would have ended." She turns away and starts walking. "Look for sympathy someplace else. I have nothing for you."

"If he finds me, you know what he'll do. You really want that on your conscience?"

Claire covers her eyes and is silent for several moments. She sighs.

"All right. I'll help you — because that's the sort of person I am. No thanks to you."

Claire reaches into her handbag and counts out some bills. She takes the woman's hand, slaps the bills into it, and pushes the hand away.

"There's a hundred dollars. That should get you a bus ticket just about anywhere. Use it to get as far away from me as you can and never come back."

The woman puts the money away. "Thank you, Chris–" She stops. "Thank you, Miss Belmonte. I appreciate it."

The woman walks off. Claire takes in several long, deep breaths and lets them out slowly. Brian steps out from behind the column just as she turns toward the door.

"You were supposed to wait inside," she says.

"Sue me," he replies. "Want to talk?"

"No."

He nods. "Well, if you do—"

"I won't. Where's this meeting?"

"Conference room in the back," Brian says, pointing toward where they need to go.

A few weeks later, while Brian and Claire are having coffee, Brian says, "Hey, that woman we saw when we went to the Jaycees, the one who called you by your middle name, is she really your mother?"

"From a biological standpoint," Claire says. "Other than that, no. She's never been. Why do you ask?"

"I saw her again."

"What do you mean, you saw her?" Claire says. "She's supposed to be miles away from here. I gave her money to leave."

"Well, either she didn't go, or she came back," Brian says. "I was out on a date with this guy and we decided to drop in at the Clermont Lounge as a goof. She was cleaning tables there. I think she works the bar, too."

"Wonderful," Claire says. "I knew I shouldn't trust her."

"She recognized me and introduced herself as Castleberry," he says.

"Irene Castleberry?" Claire says.

"I think so," he says. "Yeah, it was Irene or Ilene."

"It's Irene," Claire says. "It's her grandma's name. Figures she'd lie about that too. I do not want to have to deal with that woman again."

"I wish you could confide in me more about your past," he says.

"There's little in my past that's worth confiding about."

"That's what friends are for, you know," he says.

"Yeah. I know." She squeezes his hand. "Someday, I'll give you the whole sordid story. I promise."

Claire

Claire takes a bus to the Clermont Lounge, which is in the basement of the Clermont Hotel on Ponce de Leon in DeKalb County. It's a seedy strip club, popular with men who start drinking before noon, or college students checking it out as a joke. The strippers are much older than other clubs like the Cheetah III on Spring Street, but they don't water down the drinks, which makes no difference to Claire, since she doesn't plan to imbibe while she's there. Claire senses a palpable air of danger in the parking lot as she walks to the entrance from the MARTA stop where the bus has left her. Inside, she's nearly overwhelmed by cigarette smoke, but presses on and finds "Irene" behind the bar.

"Well, hello there, Miss Belmonte," she says. "Come for a visit or you looking for work? Don't think they're hiring dancers right now."

"What are you doing here?" Claire says. "I gave you money to leave."

"Thought I'd stick around instead. Hundred dollars don't go very far these days, you know."

"Why are you using your grandmother's name?"

"If you can be Claire Belmonte, I can be Irene Castleberry," she says. "Don't make no difference to them. They pay me in cash here."

"I want you out of this job, out of this hotel, out of this city, and above all, out of my life."

"I like it here. Made all kinds of new friends. You want me to leave, it's going to cost you a lot more than a hundred dollars, girl. Maybe you should talk to that boyfriend of yours. He looks like he might have some cash. I don't know how you snagged a good-looking fella like that."

"All it takes is one call to a certain person in Perry and it's over for you."

"Well, that's my ace in the hole, ain't it? You ain't going to contact him. You're more afraid of him than I am."

"Are you sure about that?"

"Why can't you just be happy for me?" Irene says without a lot of sincerity. "I'm reinventing myself just like you did. Now can I get you a drink or are we finished here?"

"We're done for now. But this isn't over."

"You have a nice night, then, Miss Belmonte," Irene says. "Stop back in next week if you reconsider that job offer. Girls are always leaving here. I can put in a good word for you."

"How can you be a grown man living on your own in Atlanta and not have a credit card?" Claire asks Brian as they walk to a rental car place near his apartment.

"I just never needed one before. I like to pay as I go and not have bills."

"Well they do come in handy," she says, "like, for instance, when you need to rent a car."

"I'll apply for one someday, okay? In the meantime, I sincerely appreciate your help with this."

"What do we need?"

"Something big that will get us down there and back in a hurry."

Claire opts for a Ford LTD. She lists Brian as an authorized driver.

"Since we're going that way, I need to make a pitstop in Perry," she tells him.

"Perry? For what?"

"I need to see someone about a problem I have in town."

"Does this have anything to do with that woman at the Clermont who calls you by your middle name?"

"Yeah, something like that."

Once they have the car, they hit I-75 and settle in for a long trip. Claire drives to Macon, then Brian takes over before they get on I-16.

"When we get back here, I don't want you trying to fix me up with your sister," Claire says to Brian as they travel East.

"Charlotte doesn't date women. She wouldn't be in the mess she's in now if she did."

"Well I don't either."

"So, are you celibate? I've always wondered about that, since I know you don't date men."

"I suppose you could say that," she says. "Look, I got a lot of reasons for not liking men don't have anything to do with my sexuality. One's waiting for me in Perry."

"You work around men every day," Brian says. "We're friends."

"But you're all gay. Almost every decent man I've ever known has been gay."

"So, I guess you don't worry about getting pregnant," Brian says.

"Not anymore. I can't get pregnant," Claire tells him.

"Really? Why not?"

"When I turned eighteen, I had my tubes tied."

"You did?"

"Yep," she says. "Doctor asked me if I was sure I wanted that. I told him I was never more sure of anything in my life. Still, it took a year to convince him. I finally said I was getting it done with or without him and he agreed."

"Why did you do it?" he asks.

"Just before I came to Atlanta, a man had his way with me. I was worried I'd get pregnant from it."

"Obviously, you didn't," he says.

"Nope. I tell you, there ain't no woman who was as happy to get her period as I was that following month."

"You can have it reversed, right?" he says. "What if you decide you want kids some day?"

"I don't see that happening, but I guess I'll figure it out if it ever does."

When they arrive at the house, just after dark, Charlotte is dutifully sitting on the front steps, her bags piled up on the porch behind her. Brian and Claire creep up the walkway as Charlotte rises to greet them. She throws her arms around Brian's neck and he gives her a bear hug. When he releases her, he leans in and whispers, "This is Claire."

"Claire, Claire, Claire." Charlotte takes Claire's hand and nods to her.

They load Charlotte's bags into the trunk, and as quickly and silently as they arrived, they're gone.

The following morning, the three of them are several counties over in Perry, Brian in the front seat, with Claire behind the wheel, and Charlotte asleep in the back. They are sitting across from a tiny, windowless, clapboard building with pealing, white paint, a tin roof, and a small set of steps leading to a security-barred door. On the side of the building, the word "Collections" is painted in faded black letters.

At around 7 a.m. a black, two-door, 1985 Chrysler LeBaron, in mint condition, pulls up to the office, and a small man, with dark, greying hair and a salt and pepper beard, gets out. He's wearing a plaid, buttoned down shirt and khaki pants with work shoes. He locks the car, tests the handle to be sure it's locked, then ascends the steps to the door, unlocks it and goes inside. Brian looks to see Claire, with her eyes, welling with tears, locked on the door of the office.

"Claire, who is that?" he says.

"Brian, that is the devil himself."

Brian considers this. "The devil drives a Chrysler?"

"You ever felt like you've been to Hell?" Claire asks. "Well I have been. Sixteen years under that man's roof."

"Are you sure this is such a good idea?" he says.

"If I'm ever going to be free, I got to face that devil one last time." She hands him the keys. "I think you're going to need to drive us back."

She unhooks her seat belt and opens the car door.

"Oh, here," he says as he hands her some napkins.

"Thanks." Claire dabs her eyes and checks herself in the rear-view mirror.

"If you're not out in half an hour, I'm coming in," he tells her.

"You stay here and watch over your sister," Claire says. "I'll be fine."

She gets out and straightens her clothes, then crosses the road and approaches the building. Beside the door is a weathered sign that reads, "Obadiah Carter, Certified Collections Agent, Est. 1967."

"All hope abandon ye who enter here," Claire says as she steps up to the door. She takes in a long deep breath and lets it out slowly, then enters.

The office is illuminated by a single fluorescent light fixture hanging above a metal office desk that's neatly organized. Behind it sits the man. Seeing him, Claire feels a sense of sheer panic, which she works hard to suppress. He raises his eyes to see who's come in, then stares at Claire for a long moment.

"Good morning, Miss," he says. "Is there something I can do for you?"

His calm and cold expression does not betray if he recognizes her or not. She presents herself to him.

"Good morning to you," she says with her Atlanta accent, "Zachariah."

"Well now, you know my name," he says without changing his expression. "Would that make you a repeat client?"

"My name is Claire Belmonte," she says. "Sound familiar?"

"Not at all. What is your business with me?"

She shakes her head. "Don't you even recognize me?"

"Should I?"

Claire realizes he knows very well who she is and has known since she entered. She drops her accent and leans toward him. "I always knew you weren't my daddy. You evil little man."

He fixes his stare on her as his expression darkens. "Whatever you think, young woman, my conscience is clear."

"Yeah, I know," she says returning to her Atlanta accent. "That's the problem."

Without warning, Zachariah suddenly lunges out of his seat with his hand raised. Claire takes a step back and prepares to defend herself, keeping her eyes on him. He gives her a crooked half-smile.

"Didn't shrink away from me like you used to," he says. "Guess you found your spine after all."

"I'm not afraid of you anymore," she says.

They face off for several seconds, then Zachariah sits, leans back, and links his hands in front of him.

"So, you came all this way just to tell me that," he said. "Hope it was worth the trip."

"No," she says. "I was in the area, on other business, and decided to squeeze you in."

"I appreciate you thinking of me."

"The less I think of you the better I am. Every day, I manage to exorcise a little more of you from my memory. One day, I'll be rid of you completely. But today, I've got something you want."

"What might that be?"

She reaches across his desk and takes a notepad and pen. She writes her name and number on it.

"I understand your wife's run out on you," Claire says. She sets the pad and pen onto the desk and slides the pad toward him. "You find your way to Atlanta, and call me at that number, I'll take you to her."

Zachariah takes the notepad and looks at it. "Now, why would you do that?"

She feels a lump rising in her throat, but swallows hard to suppress it. With a calm voice, she says, "As cruel as you were, she always had it within her power to relieve my suffering, and she did nothing. That's worse than what you did. She chose you over her own blood — and now she must live with that choice."

Zachariah stares at her for a long moment, then leans back and laughs heartily.

"Don't you ever say I didn't teach you nothing, girl." He tears off the note, folds it once, and places it in his shirt pocket, then tosses the pad back onto his desk and sits up. "I'm very thankful to you, Miss Belmonte. My wife's whereabouts have been a source of great consternation for me. If there's ever anything I can do to repay the favor, you know how to find me."

Claire leans on the desk and stares into his eyes. "I don't ever want to see that woman again. Think you can handle that?"

"I do believe that is within my capabilities," he says.

She straightens up. "Good. Then we'll be even. See you in Atlanta."

He nods. "You have a nice trip back, Miss Belmonte."

Claire exits, and walks back to the car. Tears are streaming down her cheeks as she gets in on the passenger side.

"Drive," she croaks at Brian.

"Sure." Brian starts the car.

Once they're on the road, she leans forward and breaks into convulsive sobs. This awakens Charlotte, who sits up and says to Brian, "Is she all right?"

"I don't know," he replies.

Claire eventually calms down but spends the rest of the trip staring out the window, saying nothing, until they pull up in front of Brian's apartment several hours later.

Before she leaves to return the car, Brian asks her, "Are you going to be okay?"

"I suppose," she says.

"I guess seeing him took a lot out of you," he says.

"It wasn't seeing him, or being in the same room with him," she replies. "It's the fact that, on some level, I gained his respect. That bothers me a lot more."

It is early evening at the Clermont Lounge. Selma Messner, still calling herself Irene Castleberry, leans on the bar and looks out at the sparse crowd. She's dressed in a sleeveless yellow blouse, baggy dungarees and work shoes, none of which are new, so she doesn't worry about spills.

A large, black woman is dancing on a platform, to the amplified sounds of "Jump" by Van Halen, surrounded by a few patrons, but otherwise business is slow. There are only a few smokers inside, but the room still reeks of cigarettes, and body odor, and beer. The real crowd won't start showing up until eight or nine, and usually later, and, on weekends, often gets younger as the evening wears on. Selma can't understand why college kids would want to hang out in a place like this, but she welcomes their tips, when they give them, and otherwise, they aren't much trouble for her. She has a little hardwood club, fashioned out of an old stool leg, positioned strategically under the bar if a patron gets too rowdy, and if things really get out of hand, she can give a sign to the bouncer and he'll handle the situation promptly.

Selma hasn't been in touch with Christine since she learned Selma was still in town and wasn't happy about it, but Selma rarely gives much currency to what her daughter wants or doesn't want. She's decided to stay on until she can think of something better to do. She doesn't make a huge salary busing tables or tending bar, but she's paid in cash, and the tips often make up for the shortfall. She's always considered herself a godly woman, but must admit, the wages of sin are sometimes quite lucrative.

Around 7:15, Selma is surprised to see Christine enter and head to the bar. Christine is usually rather sullen when dealing with Selma, but as she heads toward the bar this night, she seems to have a bounce in her step. She leans against the opposite end of the bar, a curious smile on her face, and Selma moves toward her.

"Well, hello there, Miss Belmonte," Selma says. "You here for a drink, or did you reconsider that dancing position?"

"You really like it here, don't you?" Christine says. "I never pictured you in an establishment like this."

"It ain't bad," Selma says. "I mean, the folks are usually nice, and I get some good tips. I can take it or leave it, I guess."

"You really think I'm just going to stand back and let you hang out in Atlanta?" Christine says, the curious smile still glued to her face.

"I don't see what choice you got, really," Selma says. "Ain't but one person can do anything about it, and there's no way you'd ever call him."

"Funny you should mention that," Christine says, pushing away from the counter and standing back from the bar. "Just so happens I was down that way a few days ago."

The smile on Selma's face vanishes. "No. You're lying. Ain't no way."

In response, Christine looks over her shoulder, toward the entrance. "Mr. Messner would this happen to be the person you're missing?"

There's a long pause, during which Selma almost convinces herself Christine is bluffing, then around the corner steps Zachariah.

"Why, Miss Belmonte, it is indeed," he says.

Selma can do nothing more than exclaim, "No!" She steps back from the edge of the bar and her eyes shoot to Christine. "How could you do something like this?"

"It was actually pretty easy, once I set my mind to it," Christine says, her voice slipping into the cadence of Middle Georgia. "We had a nice little chat one morning and I was moved by his sad tale. I swore I'd do all I could to reunite him with his wayward spouse."

Zachariah stares at Selma for several long seconds, then says, "Time to come on home, Selma."

Selma remains frozen behind the bar. She catches the eye of the bouncer, who walks over. "Irene, everything all right here?"

"No, it ain't," Selma says to him. "Get these people out of here. They're harassing me."

The bouncer moves so he's between Selma and the pair. "I believe the woman asked you folks to leave."

Christine looks at Zachariah, who appears on the verge of speaking. She holds up her hand to silence him. In a voice brimming with emotion, she addresses the bouncer. "Sir, this woman is my mother, and this is her husband. She's been having some mental issues, claiming to be someone she's not. I learned she ran off and was hiding out here. We're only here to try and get her the help she so desperately needs."

"Is that right, sir?" the bouncer says to Messner.

Zachariah lowers his head, and replies with deference, "Yes, sir, as embarrassed as I am to admit it. What she's said is true."

"They're lying," Selma says.

The bouncer eyes her carefully. "I suppose you have ID stating that you're who you say you are, right? I mean, that would clear things up."

Selma looks down. "Not exactly."

The bouncer looks back and forth from Selma to Christine and Messner, then throws up his hands. "I'm not getting in the middle of some domestic situation. Sorry, Irene." He walks away. Selma watches him with trepidation.

"I think that settles the matter," Christine says. "Wouldn't you agree, Mr. Messner?"

"I believe you're right, Miss Belmonte," Zachariah says. "Get your things, Selma. We've got a long drive back."

Selma lowers her head and moves out from behind the bar. "My stuff's upstairs. Won't take long." She glares at Christine. "I never imagined you could be in cahoots with him."

Christine leans in and says in a harsh voice, "Never underestimate me again."

Selma leads them outside and into the hotel. It takes her about fifteen minutes to shove all her clothing into her bags. She and Zachariah carry them down to his car.

Once Selma's seated on the passenger side, with her seatbelt on, she overhears Zachariah say to Christine. "Thank you again, Miss Belmonte. If you're ever back down our way, be sure to stop in and say hello."

"I think we both know there's not a chance in hell of that ever happening," Christine says.

Messner chuckles. "Well, all right, then. You take care of yourself, Miss Belmonte."

He gets in and drives away, leaving Christine looking after them.

Afterward

Since Brian's apartment is barely sufficient for him, the Savages have graciously offered to take Charlotte into their home. In exchange, they say, Charlotte can help out around the house and look after the kids, and they'll take care of her as her pregnancy progresses. Brian takes her over one afternoon, where Charlotte hits it off with the family, especially Gloria. In less than a week, Charlotte is behaving like one of the family. Deanna puts Charlotte in contact with resources that can help her with her spectrum disorder, and within a few months, Charlotte shows much improvement.

The following Monday after her arrival, Brian and Charlotte sign up for the open mic night at Eddie's Attic. They perform two of their collaborations and make it into the top three. For their final number, they do a new song Charlotte wrote totally on her own, with Brian making only minor suggestions on the music. They win and are invited back for the bi-annual competition in November. Charlotte proposes calling their group, Echo, and Brian agrees.

With Charlotte in town, Brian realizes he can't support himself and his sister on his salary from the restaurant, so he starts looking for other opportunities.

"You have a neighbor who works for Bickering Plummet, don't you?" Brian asks Claire.

"Half of Atlanta works for Bickering Plummet," Claire says. "My neighbor is that asshole, David Cairo."

"I remember him," Brian says. "He seemed nice enough when we spoke that one time."

"Nice? He's that jerk who's always calling me the queen of the Amazons."

"It's the same guy?" Brian says. "Look, you don't have to talk to him. Just put me in touch with him."

"Why don't you just go down there and ask if they're hiring?"

"He can tell me what they're looking for," Brian says. "Maybe give me a referral. That would be better than me walking in cold."

"I hope you appreciate all I do for you, Brian. I'll talk to Cairo when I get a chance."

David Cairo has been living one floor down from Claire's apartment for nearly two years. A native of Atlanta, he pronounces his name "Kay-ro" like the town in Georgia rather than the Egyptian city. He's in his early thirties, and works as a web developer for Bickering Plummet, a massive multinational corporation based in Atlanta, though, recently, he's been talking about starting his own web development business.

Claire has always had a contentious relationship with Cairo, with him often making playfully suggestive comments to Claire when they meet, and Claire generally reciprocating with insults, though they do have regular conversations in the laundry room, or the lobby when checking their mail. Unlike a lot of the men with whom she must deal, Cairo has always been more annoying than threatening to Claire, so she doesn't usually go out of her way to avoid him. Several inches taller than him, Claire suspects she intimidates him, though she's never tested this theory.

Even though he's one floor down from her, Claire decides not to visit Cairo's apartment, but, knowing roughly when he gets in from work, she conveniently arranges to be near the parking lot when he arrives home one afternoon. Seeing her, he throws up his hands and gives her a majestic bow.

"Greetings to you, my Queen."

"Screw you, Cairo."

"If only I was so fortunate," he says. "To what do I owe the honor of your presence, your highness?"

"I have a friend who needs a job and he asked me to find out from you if Bickering Plummet is hiring."

"Bickering's always hiring," Cairo says. "Especially with the Olympics coming up. What does your friend do?"

"Currently, he's the maître d at Coach and Six," she says.

"Sorry, Bickering's restaurant division never got off the ground," he says. "Anything else?"

"I don't know," she says. "Why don't you just talk to him?"

Cairo considers this. "I will, but only on one condition."

Claire rolls her eyes. "What's that?"

"Have dinner with me," he says. "It doesn't have to mean anything."

"Forget it," she says. "I'll just tell him to check the want ads."

"Come on," Cairo says. "Uncle Mark's playing the Attic tomorrow. It'll be fun."

"Uncle Mark," Claire says. "With Ashley?"

"I don't think they perform together anymore," he says. "But Caroline Aiken is headlining."

Claire turns away from him while she considers this.

'Okay," Claire relents, turning back. "I'll meet you there. About six?"

"Works for me," he says. "So, who's this friend?"

Cairo agrees to meet with Brian at the Starbucks near Brian's apartment. He recalls meeting Brian once with Claire a few months earlier. After some general small talk about the upcoming Olympics, and what it's like to work at Bickering, they get down to business.

"What do you do?" Cairo says, "I mean, Claire says you work at a restaurant, but what's your skill set?"

"Maître d by day," Brian says. "Singer/songwriter by night."

"Bickering isn't likely to have openings for either of those in the foreseeable future. Are you going to school?"

"Yes," Brian says. "Georgia State. Claire says you went there."

"Yeah, I got my BA there. Major?"

"Music theory and choral direction," Brian says, "with a minor in accounting."

Cairo shakes his head. "Honestly, you don't need a degree to sing or lead a choir — unless you're planning on teaching."

"That's a possibility," Brian says.

"Piece of advice from one liberal arts major to another. We always ignore the reality of the marketplace. Arts and crafts are fine, but they usually don't pay the bills."

"Okay, what do you suggest?" Brian says.

"You'll need something more business friendly if you want to work at Bickering Plummet," Cairo says. "I'd highly recommend majoring in computer science with a concentration in database management, programming, or network administration. That's where the future lies."

"I'll look into it," Brian says. "I generally do well in math and science."

"The accounting does sound promising, though," Cairo says. "They're looking for a finance manager. Have any experience running a business?"

"I managed all the finances for the choir I directed," Brian says.

"Hmm," Cairo says. "That may not be sufficient. What about facilities management? I know there's an opening which doesn't require a ton of experience."

"What would I need to do?" Brian asks.

"You know, get things fixed. Change light bulbs — stuff like that."

"I can probably handle that," Brian says.

"Are you good with paperwork?" Cairo says.

"I think so. I'm pretty organized."

"Good," Cairo says. "It's non-billable, so you won't make as much as you would as a contract worker, but I'm betting the salary will be a lot more than you're making now, and it will get your foot in the door, at least. Plus, if you're developing skills the company can use, they'll pay for your education a lot of times."

"That's all I need," Brian says.

"Once you have your degree, you can probably move over to something more lucrative," Cairo says. "Get me a copy of your résumé and switch your major."

Within weeks, Brian gets the job at Bickering Plummet, working at their downtown office, and starts looking for a larger place with an eye toward moving Charlotte in after the first of the year.

Over the summer, Charlotte gets a temp job working concessions at Olympic Stadium. This allows her to see portions of most of the track and field events when she's not working. Bickering Plummet rewards its employees with two tickets to any Olympic event and those there less than six months have their choice of several events that most people don't care about, so Brian gets to see a shooting event, and an afternoon of equestrian competition. Through a contact at the Unitarian church, Brian and Charlotte are invited to be in a choral group performing as part of the Cultural Olympiad.

Claire picks up deejay gigs at the club where she tends bar, which prompts the club owner to offer a semi-regular spot subbing for the primary deejay. Patrons seem to enjoy her mixes, but the owner tells her she needs to work on her image. This causes her to seek out Brian's advice on how she should look, not just to impress club owners and patrons, but to help her guard against people trying to take advantage of her.

"You need to seem like more of a bitch to the outside world," Brian says. "Leather, platform boots — emphasize your height — loom over people."

"You think that would help?"

"They can't take advantage of you if they're afraid to approach you," he says. "Besides, being up in the booth, you'd stand out more if you cut a larger profile."

"Good point," Claire says.

"Also, it would add some ambiguity to your look. Right now, you seem too vulnerable. For presentation, people go for more of a bad ass. You also need to work on your name."

"Way ahead of you on that," she says. "But I can't decide if I should go with Claire Christine or CC Belmonte."

Brian considers it.

"CC, definitely," he says. "Adds to the mystique. Plus, most of the deejays are guys, so it helps with the competition. They don't find out you're a woman until it's too late for them to do anything about it. Claire Christine sounds like the latest teen sensation."

"CC it is, then."

Several weeks later, David Cairo is about to let himself into his apartment when he hears a tremendous clatter on the staircase, loud clomping accompanied by what sounds like chains jangling. He pauses and is surprised when Claire appears, her hair braided in cornrows, wearing a leather biker jacket, a torn, black, T-shirt with a Black Sabbath logo, cutoff shorts, fishnet stockings, and platform boots that increase her height to nearly six and a half feet. Her jacket and boots are adorned with chains, and she's carrying a chain wallet. She stops on the landing, crosses her arms, and peers at him over the top of her aviator shades, which Cairo finds very intimidating.

"I mean you no harm, my Queen," he says, raising his hands.

"That's CC to you, Cairo," she says.

"CC?"

"CC Belmonte, deejay and sound engineer," she says.

"So, you got the job," he says. "Congratulations."

She nods and starts to clomp up the stairs toward her floor.

"Hey, did Brian tell you I'm leaving Bickering?" he calls after her.

"He mentioned it," she says. "Good luck."

On 22 January 1997, Charlotte gives birth to a healthy baby boy, who she names Edward Ishmael. Manny Savage suggests that when she's ready to go back to work, he can recommend her for a job with the Forestry Service, which meets with her enthusiastic approval. Brian has moved into a new apartment, which is large enough to accommodate Charlotte and the baby, but Charlotte finds she enjoys being with the Savages and they love having her around, so she opts to move into their tiny guest house out back. This prompts Brian to turn his place into the ultimate bachelor pad.

In the Spring of 2000, Ned Branch gets drafted out of UGA by the Atlanta Falcons. At the opening game of his first season as the backup quarterback, Echo, now a popular regional group, is invited to perform the national anthem. Afterward, they're in the skybox for the team. Lindsay Branch is there, several months pregnant. Seeing her, Charlotte goes over.

"Hey Lindsay," she says. "Been a long time."

"Charlotte," Lindsay says. "How've you been?"

"I'm getting along."

A little boy runs over to Charlotte, who lifts him up and gives him a kiss on the cheek. He looks at Lindsay and says, "Hey!"

"Hello," Lindsay says and looks him over. To Charlotte, she says, "Is he—"

"My son," Charlotte says. "Edward Ishmael. We call him Izzy."

"Edward," Lindsay says.

"That's right. He's named for his father — in more ways than one."

Charlotte puts Izzy down and he runs back to Brian.

"I suppose we're going to have to talk about it sooner or later," Lindsay says.

"We don't have to talk about it now," Charlotte says. "Y'all are living in town, aren't you?"

"We're up in Suwannee, "Lindsay says.

"Well that's just right up the road from me," Charlotte says.

"I was so angry with you for the longest time," Lindsay says.

"I was kind of angry myself," Charlotte says, "as you might imagine."

"After a while, I started asking myself why I blamed you, and couldn't come up with anything," Lindsay says. "It's really good to see you again, Charlotte."

"Same here."

"You call your group Echo," Lindsay says.

"Echo, echo," Charlotte says. "Yes, though people often think it's my name. No matter. I wear it proudly, now."

After the game, Charlotte says she needs to get Izzy home to bed, so she and Brian decide not to wait around for Ned to finish his post-game activities. Lindsay promises to have them over to their house in Suwanee, and several weeks later, they're invited up for a cookout. Ned and Izzy hit it off, and after some initial awkwardness, Charlotte and Ned agree to put the past behind them and move on. The reunion goes well, and the families agree to stay in touch. Later that year, the Branches welcome their first child, a boy they name John Isaac. Ned, Lindsay, and Charlotte agree that the boys should know one another and interact as often as possible.

Journey From Night

Rachel Lawson deals with death on a daily basis.

As a nurse who specializes in the care of terminal patients, she has experienced every aspect of a person's final days, sitting with those who are dying, consoling the spouses and loved ones, knowing the right things to say, as well as knowing when to say nothing. All who know her agree she is excellent at her job, but all her experience cannot prepare her for what she knows will be her toughest assignment. As she stares out of the window of the plane taking her from LAX to Hartsfield in Atlanta, her thoughts are of her baby sister, Sharon, and what lies ahead for her sister's young family.

It wasn't the path she'd envisioned for herself.

When Rachel graduated high school in her small town in Florida, she was considered the best-looking girl in her community, and was one of the most popular girls in her school, rivaled only by her best friend, Cherise Santiago. Cherise and Rachel had known one another practically since birth, and as they aged into beautiful young women, they remained close friends. Some jokers had taken to referring to them as Siamese twins. If one showed up, everyone knew it was only a matter of seconds before the other made an appearance. Together, they were cheerleaders, actors in school musicals, co-editors of the school paper as juniors, and of the yearbook as seniors. They dated the star players on the football team, and Rachel was idolized by most of the girls in town, most particularly by her sister, Sharon.

Rachel was considered by all who knew her to be a classic free spirit, and as beautiful as she was, she was equally kind and caring. She had the unique ability to make whoever had the pleasure of speaking with her feel like the center of the universe. Nothing, it seemed, was more important to her than spending time with that person. No one had a harsh word for her, and while the other girls envied her, no one hated her. When she and Cherise graduated, everyone agreed that if they didn't immediately go to Hollywood and become stars, the world would be a much darker place. Rachel and Cherise had lived idyllic lives, praised and pampered. For Rachel, the only dark spot was the death of her older brother, Rob, when they were children.

What most people didn't realize, but what Rachel and Cherise had known for quite a while was that they weren't simply best friends. In fact, they'd been in love with one another since at least seventh grade, though it had taken them nearly a year to acknowledge it, and at least another year to act upon that knowledge. Once they were certain, they mutually decided to keep it to themselves. The community they lived in wasn't terribly conservative, but they knew their family, friends, people in their school, and church would not understand. So, they continued to date guys, wore the class rings of their high school boyfriends, and would blush or laugh self-consciously whenever the subject of marriage came up. Neither of them could ever imagine being with someone else.

After graduation, Rachel and Cherise did as everyone expected and headed west to Los Angeles. They had no background in film and television, beyond being avid fans, and had no conception of the work involved in making it in the entertainment industry, but they had all the money they'd saved throughout high school, and as much enthusiasm as anyone could muster for a project. Most of all, they had each other, and once they arrived on the West Coast, they no longer felt constrained by their families or community and began to openly pursue their relationship. To symbolize this, Cherise designed an ornate heart, which she and Rachel had tattooed on their left shoulders, near their hearts. It was split in half, with Rachel wearing the left side and Cherise the right.

They spent a few months burning through their savings, while answering casting calls found in trade papers. They found they were no longer the most attractive women in their community, and in fact, they weren't even the most attractive in their apartment complex, and their acting skills and discipline were far inferior to the seasoned professionals they found themselves competing against. As their money began to run out, they took jobs as waitresses, first in restaurants, then in bars, and, after hearing from a fellow waitress how much money could be made in adult clubs, they began to waitress in strip clubs, and topless bars. It was here they were finally discovered.

The manager of the strip club where they waited tables took note of their looks, and how the customers responded to them, and approached them about becoming dancers. While their motto in Los Angeles had become "go with the flow", they were reluctant to pursue this suggestion, until the manager mentioned that it was a good way to break into "the business," so they auditioned. Their cheerleading and dance training served them well, and before long, both were featured performers, making several hundred dollars in tips each night. When they performed together, they made even more, being comfortable with one another as both friends and lovers. They became a popular duo at the club.

From there, they found themselves drawn into the seedy underbelly of late-70s Los Angeles, first as strippers, then "erotic" models, then "soft core" porn films and photos, simulating sexual acts with male and other female models. Finally, they graduated to "hard core" porn. Along the way, they acquired serious drug habits, using alcohol, cocaine, and heroin to quell the boredom from the "hurry up and wait" dynamic of filmmaking and the mechanical, emotionless sexual acts they performed on film. Neither of them appeared under her real name; Rachel adopted the name "Carmen Delectable" and Cherise became "Tiffany Sweetness", and they hid their identities behind wigs and tons of makeup, but they never felt comfortable with the endless stream of men and women they engaged with on camera.

As the early-80s rolled around, the porn industry was hit by a new scourge, which the doctors were calling Acquired Immune Deficiency Syndrome, and everyone else was calling AIDS. When it was still considered a "gay disease" many that appeared in hetero porn didn't think much of it, even though many actors overlapped the gay and hetero genres. Then an actress Rachel and Cherise knew was diagnosed with AIDS, and they decided it was probably best to get tested. They went in together one afternoon to a clinic near their apartment. Two days later, after Cherise was unable to join her, Rachel went back to get her results. The doctor led her into a small office and Rachel could tell from his expression that the news wasn't good.

"Ms. Lawson, I'm sorry to tell you, you've tested positive."

He went on to outline the woefully few treatment options available to patients at that time, and what she should expect as the disease began to ravage her body, but Rachel wasn't listening. The words, "you've tested positive" kept echoing in her ears, and she rose, not allowing the doctor to finish his spiel, and walked out of the clinic, as the doctor called after her, "Ms. Lawson?"

For the next forty-eight hours, Rachel did nothing but wander around L.A. in a daze. When she grew too tired to continue, she'd collapse onto a bench to rest for a while, but otherwise, she moved from point to point on autopilot, the doctor's words pounding in her head. One place was no different than the next; she neither noted nor acknowledged where she was, or what time of day it was. When she finally came out of the fog, she found herself on a beach, watching the ocean waves as they rolled in and out.

She sat, staring out at the waves, the doctor's words echoing in her mind, and imagined herself walking into the surf, walking until she could walk no further, then swimming until her arms failed her, and she was so far out, she'd have no chance of being saved. Then she'd just sink, let all the air out of her lungs, and allow her body to go under. The tide came in and splashed her bare feet and she realized she had been walking and was now just steps away from the water. It was then that the thought crossed her mind that Cherise had no idea where she was, and Rachel felt she should at least let Cherise know what was going on. Fearing what she would do if she stayed, Rachel left the beach and wandered back to the strip. It was nearly midnight.

The lights from a storefront caught her eye and as she neared it, she realized it wasn't a shop, but a small church. Feeling she could use some divine intervention, Rachel went inside, where she found a man with long hair and a full beard, and not much older than she was. He introduced himself as the pastor. He sensed something was wrong, and asked her to sit and invited her to share what had brought her in. She sat with him for several hours, pouring out her heart, telling him of where her life had taken its wrong turn, and finally, of the doctor's words at the clinic. The pastor embraced her and assured her that she had a home there, and encouraged her to return to Cherise, to let her know Rachel was alive.

Cherise had discovered that afternoon that the clinic had mixed up their records. They went in together to be tested, but Rachel had gone back alone, and the attendant handed the doctor Cherise's results by mistake. When Cherise showed up, the doctor realized the mix-up, and after giving Cherise the devastating news, compounded it by telling her that he'd mistakenly told Rachel she had AIDS. So now, in addition to learning she would most likely die, she had the added burden of worrying what had happened to Rachel.

Rachel returned to the apartment and found Cherise in tears.

"What is it?" Rachel said, taking Cherise into her arms.

"I have AIDS."

"You too?"

Cherise pulled away from Rachel and took her hands. "No. There was a mistake. You're okay. They mixed up the results."

The fleeting moment of relief Rachel felt was eclipsed by the sorrow she felt over Cherise's news.

"Listen to me," Rachel said. "I'm going to take care of you, okay? I don't care how bad things get. I'll be there for you."

Rachel was as good as her word. She took Cherise to the church she'd found, and they joined and became very active. They gave up the drugs and booze and committed their lives to spending as much time together as possible. As Cherise's health declined, Rachel devoted herself to caring for her, and when Cherise got to the point Rachel could no longer deal with her at home, she got Cherise into the best hospice she could find and became a volunteer so they could be together. A supervisor there noted Rachel's care and compassion for the patients and suggested nursing might be a good career for her, so after Cherise died in early 1990, Rachel took the advice and pursued nursing. She found the one area she could have the most impact was in caring for those facing death. The once vibrant party girl who always chose to "go with the flow" had grown into a thoughtful, introspective, and spiritual woman, who projected an overwhelming sense of calm.

Then Rachel received the most devastating news since learning of Cherise's condition. For nearly a year, her sister Sharon had been complaining about being tired and listless. Despite Rachel's admonitions, Sharon had put off seeing a doctor, focusing instead on her children, Rebecca and Steven. When she finally went in for a checkup, she learned that she had advanced ovarian cancer, which was spreading rapidly. Upon hearing this, Rachel quit her job, informed her landlord she'd be leaving and boarded a plane to Atlanta. Rachel knows very well what's in store for her sister, and she isn't going to let Sharon, Rebecca, and Steven face it alone.

A Debt to Pay

Annabelle Collins wheeled herself out to the back porch of her home in Kirkwood and watched as Paul Searcy continued his yard work. As she watched him work, she again experienced the mixed feelings his presence brought to her. He looked in her direction and gave his customary nod.

"Afternoon, ma'am," he said.

In all the time she'd known him, he had never called her by her first name. It was always "Miss Collins" or "ma'am." Annabelle didn't mind. She liked the formality of their relationship, as it provided her the appropriate amount of distance from him. Distance was important to Annabelle, particularly when it came to Paul.

"Hello, Paul," she replied. "The garden's coming along nicely, I see."

"Yes, ma'am," Paul said before resuming work.

Annabelle went back inside and maneuvered around the furniture of the living room to get to her computer. To one side was a pile of student essays waiting to be graded, but Annabelle ignored them and went on the Internet, checking her email, then her Facebook account. Finding nothing that interested her, she rolled away from her desk and wheeled around so she could view Paul through the back window. He was tall, and his upper body was well developed, and he went about his tasks quickly and energetically. By all measures, he was an attractive man, polite and soft-spoken, and loyal to a fault. Still, Annabelle regarded him with ambivalence, never quite able to get past how they had become acquainted, the reason he was now a part of her life full-time.

As a young man, Paul, the son of a prominent business owner in Kennesaw, Georgia, had been reckless and impulsive. He held fast to his unsupported belief that he would not live long and decided to party as much as possible. By the age of twenty-two, he was well-known to the local police for a variety of minor offenses, mainly involving alcohol or disturbing the peace, but he was generally thought of as more of a threat to himself than others, and his family's influence was usually enough to settle any problems that arose. One evening, while drinking heavily he hopped into his truck and headed off to purchase more beer.

That's what brought him to the same cross-street in Cobb County, where Annabelle, in her senior year at Spelman College, had just gotten the green light, and headed into the intersection turning left. She was going to a party in Marietta, and didn't notice the dark pickup barreling toward her, until it ran the light and T-boned her car at the driver-side door.

When she awoke in the hospital several weeks later, she was greeted by the news that her spine was severed just above her waist. She'd never walk again and might never be able to live an independent life. Annabelle had been on the track team at Carver High School and was a star athlete at Spelman. The news nearly destroyed her.

In the meantime, Paul had been arraigned and was sitting in jail, his father refusing to put up the money to bail him out. What he could remember of the accident played over and over in his head, and he wondered if he should just save the state the money for his trial and find some way to end his life right then and there. But something happened to Paul in that cell. For the first time in his life, he decided to take responsibility for his actions. He instructed the lawyer the court appointed for him not to fight the charges. He would plead guilty, accept the maximum sentence the superior court of Georgia chose to give him, which ended up being fifteen years, and he'd do the time, which is what he did. Inside, he became a model prisoner, earned a degree, learned a trade, and was the perfect candidate for early release, but every time the subject of parole came up, Paul refused to consider it.

Annabelle defied her doctors' expectations, and successfully underwent rehabilitation, learning to get around in the chair that now took the place of her legs. While she was able to regain her mobility, she'd lost her spirit and more importantly, she lost her faith. Before the accident, Annabelle, the daughter of a well-respected minister in the African Methodist Episcopal Church, was wavering in her beliefs, but afterward, she abandoned her faith altogether, believing no just god would punish its followers as she had been.

As she gained enough freedom of movement to allow her to leave her parents' home and get an apartment by herself, she also began to retreat from the world. She did not return to school and became withdrawn from those who'd known her all her life. Once she was in her own place, she stopped attending services at her father's church. At first, he constantly questioned her about this, until she emphatically told him why she wasn't returning. It cast a pall over their relationship for the remainder of his life.

She rarely left her apartment, rarely had visitors and most of her "friends" were people she met online. Not even her family had been there often, beyond the time they helped her move in, and usually the only time her parents, brothers or sister saw her was when she made her infrequent visits home, usually preceded by a call asking her father to pick her up. She completed her degree through computer coursework and settled into a job as a medical transcriptionist, lonely work, staring at a computer screen all day. The bulk of her time when she wasn't working was spent surfing the Internet, interacting with people she did not know and had little desire to meet in person. Eventually, she earned enough to afford a house in Kirkwood, which is where Paul found her after being released from prison.

When he first thought about visiting her, he wrestled with the decision for several weeks. He knew she probably wouldn't want to see him, and so, when he made the decision to proceed, he didn't call her to set up a meeting; he just looked up her address and made plans to stop by some afternoon. He had no idea how she'd dealt with the aftermath of the accident. Other than her presence in court on the day of his sentencing, he'd not seen nor spoken to her and then she'd been silent, staring blankly at him conveying nothing of how she felt.

On a trip outside to get her mail, Annabelle noted a white man about her age standing at the bus stop a few houses down and something about him seemed familiar to her, but she concluded that he must be someone from the neighborhood and paid him little attention. She hardly knew any of her neighbors, so she had no idea who belonged and who didn't. After she'd gone back inside, ten or fifteen minutes passed before the doorbell rang and she was surprised to find the same man at her door. As was her custom, she'd locked the iron security door outside, so when she opened the front door, she knew there was a safe barrier between her and her visitor.

"Can I help you?" Annabelle said.

"Miss Collins, I'm Paul Searcy."

It took a moment for the years to fade away, but suddenly she was again looking at the face of the man who'd put her in that chair. He looked a good deal more mature than the disheveled twenty-two-year-old who'd sobbed as he repeated, "I'm sorry. I'm really sorry," from the witness stand at his sentencing. She had not reacted at the time, still emotionally numb from the experience, unlike her father, who took Paul to task for his actions and urged him to "get right with God." In the intervening time, she had come to regard the scene with contempt, feeling his whole show of guilt was an act put on for the court.

Now, he stood before her, much taller than she remembered him, with a military-style buzz cut, his shoulders back and looking at her with his head turned slightly away from her.

"I remember you. What do you want?" she said coolly.

"I was hoping I could talk to you a moment."

"I honestly don't think there's anything for us to talk about," she said. "I wasn't even aware you were out of prison."

"Yes, ma'am," he replied. "I was released last year."

"Isn't someone supposed to notify the victims?" she said. "Should you even be here? I mean, aren't you violating your parole or something?"

"I'm not on parole, ma'am," he said. "I served the full term. I guess they figured I paid my debt to society."

"That's really nice to know," she said, a note of sarcasm evident, "I'm really proud of you. Now, if you'll excuse me—"

She started to close the door, but Paul put up his hand.

"Miss Collins, please, I'd really like to have a few words with you," he said. "I promise you I'm not here to harm you—"

"More than you already have?" she spit back at him.

"That's fair, I suppose," he replied, looking down. "I just have a few things to say to you and once I'm done, I'll leave and won't bother you again. I swear."

Annabelle stared at him a long moment. Seeing him brought back a rush of emotions she thought she'd buried, and her first instinct was to slam the door and call the police. Something in how Paul presented himself suggested to her he was sincere, however, so despite her misgivings, she unlocked the security door and rolled back into the living room, allowing him to enter.

"Ten minutes," she said, "and if I tell you to go, you go — understand?"

"Of course," he said. He went to the couch and sat.

"How'd you get here anyway? I didn't see a car."

"I don't drive, ma'am," he said. "They told me I could probably get my license back, but I'd rather not get behind the wheel again, unless I have to."

"That's good news," Annabelle said. "So, what is it you need to tell me?"

"I wanted to see how you were," he said, "how you're getting along."

Annabelle spread out her arms.

"Still paralyzed," she said. "I'm not running anymore, obviously. Spelman didn't have a Paralympic team. Is that all?"

"No, ma'am," he said. "I've had a lot of time to think the last fifteen years. I've always tried to imagine what I'd say if I got the opportunity to talk to you— I guess now that I'm here, the words are a little hard to come by."

"Time is short, so make something up," Annabelle said.

Paul stared at her a moment, then chuckled.

"What?" Annabelle said.

In response, Paul reached into his pocket and removed a photo which he held out for Annabelle to take.

"I was just thinking you haven't changed all that much," he said.

She rolled over and took it from him, finding it to be a photo of her from college.

"Where did you get this?" she said.

"Your father," he said. "About a month after I went to prison, he visited and gave it to me."

"My father went to see you," she said holding up the photo, "and gave you this?"

"Yes, ma'am," he said. "He told me he wanted me to always have a reminder of what I'd done — like I could ever forget."

She handed the photo back and rolled away from him. "That sounds like my father."

"He was a rather formidable man, I recall," Paul said. "I understand both your parents are deceased, my condolences."

"How do you know that? Have you been stalking me?" she said. "Maybe it's time for you to go."

"No, ma'am," he said, sliding to the edge of the couch, "it's not like that. I ran across their obituaries when I was trying to find your address."

"Oh. Okay. Well your time is running out none-the-less," she said with urgency in her voice. "So, whatever you have to say, just say it."

Paul nodded. "As I say, I've had a lot of time to think about what I did. I've always wished there was some way I could make it up to you, but I realize nothing I do is going to be sufficient. I thought, maybe if I saw you, talked to you, I'd be able to think of some way to help."

Annabelle shook her head and sighed loudly.

"I get it. This is some sort of twelve-step thing where you go around asking for forgiveness from all the people you've hurt.

Well sorry, Paul. I'm all out of pity."

"I don't want your pity, or your understanding, or your forgiveness," he said. "I don't deserve any of that. Your father said he'd pray for my redemption, but I told him not to. I've never forgiven myself for what I did. I never will. If you hate me, I don't blame you. I don't deserve anything else."

"Then what do you want?" she asked.

He lowered his head. "I took your life away from you. I'm here to offer you mine."

Annabelle stared at Paul for a long time, totally caught off guard by what he had just said to her.

"Are you saying you want me to kill you?" she finally said.

"No, ma'am," he replied. "I want you to use me."

"Use you for what?"

"Whatever," he said. "Maybe you need work done around here. Maybe there's something you can't do. Whatever you need."

Annabelle again shook her head.

"Unbelievable," she said to him. "You think you can come in here and do a few odd jobs and everything will be okay between us."

"You're not understanding what I'm telling you, ma'am," he replied. "I'm not talking about doing a little work for you. I'm talking about being there for you, for whatever reason, from here on out."

"You mean, like a servant?" she said.

"If that's what you need, yes," he told her. "If you just need somebody to fix things, or build things, or just someone to talk to, I can do that, too. Whatever."

Annabelle considered his words for a long moment.

"I think, if I'd ever tried to imagine how this meeting would go, this would have been the last thing I'd have come up with," she finally said. "What makes you think I'd even want you around here? You went to prison? You paid your debt? Well guess what, you got out." She indicated the chair. "I'm still there because of you and I'll never get out."

She rolled away from him then turned to face him again.

"And now you expect me to have you around my house? Working here for who knows how long? My god! The mere fact that you're still sitting there, that I haven't gone into my room and gotten my baseball bat and beaten your brains out is a testament to the remarkable level of restraint I'm showing you now."

"I appreciate that, ma'am," Paul said with some hesitation. "Maybe I'm stupid for coming here, but I had to do something."

"I don't even know what to say at this point," she replied. "I am officially stunned into silence."

They both fell silent. Annabelle took the opportunity to examine Paul. She'd carried the image of the remorseful young man around with her ever since the trial, but the man who sat across from her now seemed completely different, calmer, and more thoughtful. Since the time of his emotional pronouncement at his sentencing, she had never believed him to be sincere, but now, looking at him, she began to suspect he might be telling her the truth, that he truly wanted to make amends for what he'd done.

Still, she had no reason to trust him.

As she considered what her response would be, Paul glanced at his watch and rose.

"Well, I guess that's ten minutes. I appreciate you taking the time to hear me out."

"Wait, you're really just going to leave?"

"I told you I would."

He started toward the door.

"You're a man of your word," Annabelle said after him.

"Excuse me?" Paul turned back toward her.

Annabelle wheeled around so she was looking at Paul.

"I could use a ramp," she said.

"A ramp?"

"The only way I can get out back is to go out the front and around the driveway," she said. "If I had a ramp to the back porch, I could go out the back."

Paul considered it.

"I learned some carpentry in prison," he said. "I could do that."

Annabelle nodded.

"After that, we'll see," she told him. She rolled toward him then pointed, "But understand this. I am not your friend. I am not your charity case. When I need something, I'll let you do it, but otherwise, keep your distance."

"Yes, ma'am," Paul said. "I can start tomorrow if that's okay with you."

Annabelle nodded. "That's fine. From here on out, consider yourself on probation."

"Yes ma'am."

That had been nearly ten years ago and twenty-five since Paul first entered her life. Having him around had been difficult at first, but the more he was there, the more she grew accustomed to having him there. She eventually let him rent the small studio in her basement, so he could be around if she needed any help in the evenings. He kept the house and yard well-maintained as well as keeping her company, and over time he had become a reassuring presence in her life. A year or so after he moved in, Annabelle purchased a van with handicapped controls, so she could drive again, which helped with buying groceries and supplies. Sufficiently mobile, she began work at Spelman for a doctorate in Literature and was later hired as an adjunct professor.

She was not sure she would ever consider herself to be Paul's friend, and she was pretty sure she could never forgive him, but, at least, she knew she could trust him, and for Annabelle, that was all that mattered.

Dead Man's Hat

Inspired by "Small Change" by Tom Waits

Lenny heard the shots. Hell, everybody on the block heard the shots, but nobody saw anything. Nobody ever saw anything, not even those who were there, looking right at whatever was happening. They were the ones who especially didn't see anything because they knew what would happen to them if they did. Lenny knew, so he made an extra effort to not see anything. Like when he saw Artie go by and enter the arcade. Lenny knew it was only a matter of time before he'd need to look away. So, he did.

Arthur Desanto had been in town for about a week, from Chicago, he claimed. Lenny hadn't met many people from Chicago. He'd get a lot of New Yorkers asking him if he knew where they could find the Times, but Artie was the first one from Chicago, or at least the first to say so. Artie got really quiet when Lenny asked why he was in Atlanta, and Lenny knew not to press him. Other than that, Artie had been pretty talkative, asking about the night life, such as it was. Lenny told him about the San Souci and the Domino, but Artie had already found them and didn't seem too impressed. There was also the Clermont over on Ponce, which Lenny mentioned to Artie.

Artie was staying in the Grady Hotel, which was why Lenny had the opportunity to get to know him a bit. Artie never seemed to have anything to do from two to four, so he hung out near the diner, chewing an enormous wad of gum and quizzing Lenny about baseball players on cards he had in his pocket. Artie was a collector, he said, though Lenny couldn't figure out why anybody would want to hang on to those things once the gum was gone. As a kid, Lenny had been a fan of the Crackers and went to games with his father when they played on Ponce but didn't follow the sport on a national level. He didn't know much about this new team they brought in from Milwaukee and hadn't yet been out to the stadium they built for them south of town last year. Artie was fairly knowledgeable, but Lenny got the strong sense Artie was just showing off, which didn't really impress Lenny all that much, but he didn't want to seem rude. Lenny figured Artie just needed someone to talk to and Lenny didn't have a whole lot to do until the afternoon edition came out anyway.

Lenny was a news boy, hawking the Journal in the afternoons on Peachtree between Ellis and Cain Streets downtown. He'd been doing it for about a year, among other odd jobs, after dropping out of Brown High School to help his Mom make ends meet following his father's death. Lenny was the oldest of two boys and two girls, so he saw it as his responsibility to step up once his father was gone. He liked working for the Journal, even if he was just selling papers, because his dream was to be a writer, covering the mean streets of his hometown of Atlanta. Because of this, he always kept his eyes and ears open, and only turned away when he knew it was in his best interest to do so. He liked to study people, how they dressed, how they carried themselves. He could usually guess someone's profession by what that person was wearing and working outside a hotel he encountered a fine mix of people from all over.

What caught Lenny's eye when he first saw Artie was the hat. A porkpie, they were called, dark brown and made of felt — not the sort of hat one usually saw around Atlanta, which is why it made such an impression on Lenny. He never saw Artie without it, not even when Artie was in the diner, eating. He didn't take the hat off or hang it up like other guys would do. It was always perched atop his head, like Artie expected to run out at any minute and didn't want to risk leaving it behind.

Artie was a nervous sort, small and wiry, and not much taller than Lenny, who, at sixteen, was just a hair over five nine. During one of their discussions, Artie let it slip that in Chicago, he was known as "Small Change" and Lenny felt the nickname suited Artie, who seemed small and unimportant, the sort most would pass by unless he gave them a reason to stop. Beyond that, Lenny had no idea what Artie did for a living, if anything, and Artie wasn't the sort to volunteer the information.

In the aftermath, people would say Artie was an idiot, thinking he could run to Atlanta and be safe. Nobody was safe in Atlanta, but most of them didn't know it. Artie knew it. He wasn't safe anywhere. There are just some folks you don't mess with and the consensus was that Artie should have known that. Lenny was never a hundred percent sure exactly what Artie had done or to whom, but whoever it was wasn't the sort to forgive and forget.

Artie seemed to sense the end was coming. Each day when he'd stop and talk, he'd seem more nervous: looking over his shoulder, asking if anyone had been inquiring after him. Once, when a car backfired, he practically jumped out of his skin.

Whatever it was, he wasn't telling Lenny. "The less you know, my friend, the less you know," Artie would repeat, often without prompting from Lenny.

Both the Constitution and Journal fudged the details of the crime, stating only that Artie had been shot multiple times by an unknown assailant, most likely a robbery gone wrong. Lenny had seen him, though, sprawled on the ground, his head resting against the base of a gum ball machine. Lenny knew the real story — five shots, one in each shoulder, one in each knee, then the final one between the eyes, with a single, unspent cartridge beside his head. Everybody on the streets knew whose signature that was, even the cops. Nobody could prove it, though, and that was the show stopper.

The kicker was, whoever did the deed used Artie's own gun, the .38 snub nosed revolver he kept in his coat pocket, which was found, empty, a few feet from the body. Lenny imagined Artie going for it but being a couple of seconds too late. The type of men he was facing needed to be surprised to get the drop on them. It takes a special kind of man to look someone in the eye then shoot him multiple times and Artie just wasn't the type. The guy who killed Artie probably went home, had a nice dinner with the wife and kids, and never gave it a second thought.

Lenny was halfway down the block, just a few yards away from the entrance to the arcade when it all went down. He'd seen Artie nervously head inside, after ignoring Lenny's usual greeting, "Hi ya, Artie," as he passed. Lenny had also seen the man in the black suit and the grey fedora pass by with two other fellows dressed less formally, who entered the arcade behind Artie. He'd seen the flow of teenagers leaving quickly and that's when he knew it was time to turn away, to focus on something else for a few minutes, until he knew all was clear.

It took maybe five minutes, but then the shots came and the three men who'd followed Artie exited, not in any hurry, and passed Lenny as they headed to the end of the street. One of them even stopped to buy Lenny's last paper, and waved off the change Lenny offered him, with a cool, "Keep it, kid," before they disappeared around a corner.

Then the buzzards descended, Wally from the shoe shine stand, Hazel from the coffee shop next door, Frankie from the clothing store across the street. They grabbed what they could easily remove from the body and beat it quickly. By the time Lenny got there the corpse had been picked clean, no watch, no wallet, no cufflinks or ring. But there was one thing left, and, for Lenny it was the prize. Lying just to the right of the body, away from the quickly spreading pool of blood was the hat, where it must have fallen when Artie reacted to the first shots, or maybe while the men were "talking" with Artie beforehand. Lenny stepped over and picked it up, examined it to be sure there was no trace of blood, then walked to the mirror and tried it on. He'd need to grow into it, but he had to admit, it looked pretty good on him.

Lenny straightened his jacket and walked out of the arcade wearing the hat. He breathed in the early evening air, then turned right and headed south, just as the first of the police cruisers rounded the corner with sirens blaring and lights flashing. Lenny didn't stop. Nobody had seen him going in or coming out. Nobody ever saw anything.

He had no idea how the situation would eventually be resolved, but he knew he was going to write about it. In two years, after all the commotion had died down, he'd turn it into a human-interest piece about life and death in the city, which would become the first byline in the Journal for Leonard Stringer. As he strolled away from the scene, words began to form in his head.

"Small Change — rained upon with his own .38," he thought and nodded with satisfaction. He shoved his hands into the pockets of his jacket and headed off to the Journal to collect his day's pay, with a slight bounce in his step.

Remains

I'll state up front, she dies — eventually. I mean, we all do, right? Nothing any of us can do will make much of a difference. I don't want people getting a false sense of hope that things work out between us in the end because they don't. They almost never do, really.

I won't use the "real" name she gave me because that person needs to remain hidden, alive or not. No one ever saw the woman behind the image and she made that as clear as she could, through both her music and things she told me. If she's still using a stage name, I don't know it. Even if I did, I wouldn't tell.

The name people recognized was Shayna Banks, but that was an illusion she created that has served its purpose. It kept people from asking too many questions. She didn't like questions and unlike some wasn't very good at hiding her disdain.

Perhaps I should start at the beginning, or as close as I can come to the beginning since I came in part-way through her story.

Imagine walking into a club and hearing a voice so enticing that it consumes every fiber of one's being. That was her. She was standing at the mic, holding a guitar and pouring out her soul for the mostly indifferent crowd: pool players, folks there to watch the game, drinkers, smokers, all contributing to the general din, with no idea what a miracle they were missing.

I took a seat near the stage — there were a lot — and gave her my undivided attention. I think she sensed someone was there to listen because her sound brightened a bit. I guess I came in just after she started, because she played for another twenty or thirty minutes.

Afterward, we talked for a while and I got on her contact list and bought a CD. Many artists sound different in the studio than live but as I listened to her CD in the car, I was pleased to hear that recording her voice had not diminished its power.

From that point on, I saw her wherever she played locally, and once, on a whim, I drove all the way to Birmingham to see her, which surprised her to no end. It was just after the Birmingham show where I gained her trust, if not her friendship.

She rode up with some fellow musicians, including the driver who apparently wanted to get to know her on a more intimate level. When she made it clear to him after the show that it wasn't going to happen, he drove off and left her at the venue. I was the only other person she knew who was headed back to Atlanta, so after several protests about the inconvenience, she agreed.

At first, as we rode along, I tried to get some personal info out of her, but my inquiries were met with silence. Instead, we started talking about music and that's where she opened up. She had eclectic influences: Blues, Jazz, Sixties Rock, but she also mentioned Broadway musicals that her mother had introduced to her via soundtracks played around the house. We had a good talk, and as I dropped her off, she told me to let her know when I was coming to a show, so she could put me on "the list".

Understand, we were never friends, as that would have required a level of openness on her part that she wasn't willing to give, but after Birmingham she trusted me, and to her, trust was more important than friendship. Truth be told, she was linked to a lot of people, women, men, the evidence was never definitive on her preference, or if she even had one. She never told me, and I never asked.

After she was gone, a number of people claimed to have been with her. I suppose it's a game. If one can't be special, then attach oneself to someone who is, regardless of whether it's true or not. If there were no witnesses, who's to say after the fact?

She was "successful" I suppose, at least by industry standards. She started selling some records, booking larger venues, touring. She never liked the attention, but she loved the connection, standing in front of the audience, hearing them sing along to one of her songs. She told me once that she missed the intimacy of smaller venues, where she could talk to people after shows.

She recorded quite a bit and was always in the studio or at a concert. She didn't quite make it to the status of headliner, during her brief time in the spotlight, but she was always an anticipated opening act, and always a big draw when she played occasional solo shows at favored local spots.

I asked her about it once and she denied she was successful. She didn't equate being well-known or selling records with success. "It's the music," she told me. "If it doesn't mean anything, what else matters?" For every song she recorded, there were probably ten others she'd written that the label decided wasn't commercial.

If I had to speculate on what drove her to what she did, I'd have to guess it was the loss of her freedom. It's what caused her to take a hiatus, just at the point where many felt she was about to have her big breakthrough. She just put on the brakes and retired to her cabin in the woods, "to reassess".

No one is certain exactly what happened. The best guess based on the evidence collected is that she simply went for a hike in the woods near her house one day and never came back. There wasn't anyone checking in on her, so several weeks passed before anyone even thought to miss her. Her behavior had not seemed out of the ordinary leading up to the last time anyone heard from her and it was normal for her to go several days, weeks even, without any communication as long as she had all her necessities nearby. She often remarked how much she liked getting lost in nature and how convenient it was living near a forest.

When she missed a show at a popular venue the show runner went to her place and called the police when he couldn't get anyone to come to the door. For several weeks after, there were searches and APBs, and her photo was flashed across the country. She became more famous after her disappearance than she'd been before, and the record company took full advantage of that by promoting her back catalog. Sales of her music tripled. No one knew her well enough to say what might have been on her mind, so no one could speculate on what happened to her.

Some months later a couple of hikers in the woods near her place stumbled across what turned out to be a human femur. A search of the area turned up additional bones, including a skull, that were scattered as though predatory animals had gotten at the body. The skull was missing about half its teeth, but enough bones were found to reveal they belonged to a female about her age and height. Nearby were fragments of clothes which matched items she'd typically wear. For most who followed the situation, that was all that was needed to close the books.

She didn't leave much behind beyond her household supplies. The most important item was what she called her goodie bag, the knapsack full of personal effects she took the pains to haul around with her everywhere she went. She said it contained her remains. Inside was a high school yearbook, two pairs of well-worn, lace-up checkerboard Vans, a pair of men's jeans, and an old cigar box that contained these items:

- Her high school class ring
- A photo of her mother
- A handwritten list of phone numbers most of which go to disconnected lines
- A couple of napkins bearing the names of local bars, both now closed

- A sheet containing lyrics to the first song she ever wrote — a note says at age ten
- An invitation to her high school graduation
- A flash drive containing her video diary entries, none of which reveal very much
- An unsigned, undated note on lined paper that reads, "Why, Daddy, why?"

There was also this poem, written on the back of one of her promotional cards, and undated; the word "Songbird" was scribbled, sideways, beside it:

Lone on the road another year.
Don't look back
no time to cry.
Tell the tales
they wish to hear.
Play the pleasing music once again.

Tear your heart out
make them smile.
They own you now, you know.
They put you in
your gilded cage
and they possess the key.

Primp your feathers
now's the time.
Tortured songbird,
prisoner of the road.
Break the silence
give the pleasure.

It all begins again next year.

Did these represent the sum total of her life — items she felt she needed with her, right up to the point where she left them behind at a place that she considered to be her home? I do believe she deliberately left them there, because I think she knew she wasn't coming back.

See, I saw the skull they found — she didn't have many friends, but I was counted as one, which gained me access — anyway I examined it and while there were only a few teeth left in it, two of them had fillings. I know for a fact she had never had any dental work done. She told me that herself, even showed me when I doubted her.

So, I don't know who the poor soul was whose skull they found, but it wasn't her. Don't believe me? Then consider: to this day, no one has found her notebooks in which she wrote all her songs. They vanished with her.

I don't know why she left her stuff behind. Maybe she thought she wouldn't need it anymore. Maybe there's more to be found in the woods, since they cover a lot of acres. Maybe she just needed her disappearance to be convincing. I have it if she ever reappears though I doubt she ever will. Whether she's alive or dead, she was done with that portion of her life.

Still, I'll hang on to it for her, just in case.

Bare-Assed Messiah

One might think that a naked man walking down Peachtree Street in Atlanta in the afternoon would be easy to spot, but Doyle Pendergast wasn't the typical naked man. He strode along with confidence, almost daring anyone to call him out. He made eye contact, greeted those who bothered to notice him with a boisterous, "Howdy!" If hands were offered, he'd vigorously shake them before continuing on his way. If anyone took exception with his state, he'd cease his forward movement and engage the aggrieved party in a lengthy discourse about what he was doing and why, and few who questioned him found fault with his reasoning.

In this way, he devised a curious form of invisibility. People deliberately didn't see him, giving him license to make his daily treks largely unhindered. Even the police steered clear, not wanting to explain to their superiors how such an individual had been able to move with impunity for so long through their streets.

It was almost by chance that Doyle first began his odd excursions. Before, he'd been the typical office drone, working in just another cubicle city in another unadorned office building, at the downtown branch of Bickering Plummet, Inc. He had been with his employer more years than he wanted to count and, while he progressed over time, never really felt rewarded for his endeavors. He'd started as a low-level clerk, fresh out of college and, over time, managed to rise to a low-level office support representative, spouting his practiced spiel whenever someone would call for assistance.

Doyle was behind-the-scenes, hardly noticed unless someone needed his assistance, and, for a long time, he relished the anonymity. Beneath the surface, however, there was always this wild streak to his personality, which he mostly suppressed, the longing to break out and do something totally unconventional, something no one expected. Which is why, one afternoon, completely out of the blue, he decided to remove his shirt while he was headed home from work.

The thought first struck him in the lobby of his office building, an impulse he found difficult to resist. In fact, it happened almost unconsciously, as he strode away from the elevator toward the door; he just started undoing the buttons of his shirt, so that by the time he exited through the revolving doors, his shirt was slung over his shoulder. He assumed this would cause a stir, people staring, not able to comprehend why this man had suddenly decided to go shirtless, but, to his surprise, no one seemed to care. People glanced in his direction, but no one made much of a fuss about it, which further inspired him.

From there it was a simple matter to remove more and more clothing, until he was moving along completely in the buff, once again expecting to shock the unsuspecting masses, and once again finding himself all but completely ignored. He was somewhat disappointed at first, until he realized that in not reacting to him, the people downtown were giving him the biggest reaction of all. The more they tried to ignore him, the more he found them making furtive glances in his direction, then abruptly turning away, pretending not to have seen what they had, in fact, just seen. He knew he'd hit upon his one grand gesture. Now he considered himself an artist.

Eccentricity was no stranger to Doyle's family. His cousin Cecilia, who lived in North Georgia, was part of a religious organization called The First Church of Jesus Christ, Steno, or The Christian Stenographers. Founded on the Internet in the early 90s, their mission in life was to faithfully record every word Jesus said to them for later revelation, and they frequently issued voluminous correspondence on every topic imaginable. The Evangelicals, fearing the competition, immediately set out to discredit them, calling them a cult and instructing members to ignore the lengthy, often cryptic epistles issued by the group. What really worried the clergy was a larger concern: namely, what if these yahoos actually were receiving messages directly from Jesus? Where would that leave the rest of them?

Cecilia Baskin was once a well-respected court reporter, who was active in her church, and a frequent volunteer outside her home. She was also a proud member of the Clan Baskin and participated in every family gathering in full Scottish regalia; but that was before she began to have problems leaving her house. She could never vocalize exactly what it was that frightened her about being outside, just that every time the thought arose of going out, she'd be overcome with abject terror, and a sense of foreboding that something terrible would happen. Within a year, she went from being a vibrant, friendly, and active participant in life, to a sullen shut-in, who wouldn't even answer the door unless the given signal had been given, indicating it was her sister-in-law bringing her groceries and other necessities. Most of her time was spent scribbling shorthand into her notepad or caring for her cats, and she rarely entertained family or friends any longer.

Finding her new "church" online had been a beacon of light to Cecilia, and she dove into this new endeavor, where she could use her reporting skills, with a new-found passion. Doyle had, with increasing frequency, received her curious epistles, as had most in their family, but he rarely gave them more than a cursory glance, maybe managing the first or second paragraph before skipping to his next email. Now that he'd taken on his own mission to engage the world, he started to take a second look at his cousin's correspondence and found them very insightful.

Most were written in a rambling, stream of consciousness style, one thought hardly connected to the next, but through them all, Doyle noted a keen sense of logic, encased in a vast array of religious symbolism. Cecilia's emails were always twenty-five hundred words, no more, no less, and each new email took up where the last left off, as though she was instinctively editing pages and pages of her handwritten notes, knowing just where to stop and start. Though each was a long stream of words, they were perfectly punctuated and capitalized. The sentences varied, giving a cadence to the notes as though they'd been meant to be read aloud; sometimes, Doyle did just that, finding them to be clever monologues, if somewhat nonsensical ones. If only he could find a way to connect them to his afternoon excursions, he was certain he could make people sit up and take notice. He might even realize his life-long dream of being interviewed on Action News.

To put his plan into play, Doyle first had to pay a visit to his cousin, since he had purged a large volume of her correspondence. This proved challenging, because Cecilia would not answer the door to anyone she was not expecting and would not invite anyone to her home she didn't know well. She and Doyle had hardly interacted since they were children, even when Cecilia was in a better frame of mind. He not only did not know how to contact her directly, he wasn't even sure which of his relatives had stayed in direct touch with her, so he was at a total loss as to how to approach her. He contacted his sister, who put him in touch with a distant cousin, who eventually narrowed down Doyle's search to Glenda, the wife of Samuel, his third cousin, once removed; Glenda, it was said, visited Cecilia on a regular basis and shopped for her.

Doyle first formulated what his cover story would be, then, satisfied with what he'd devised, phoned his cousin Samuel — who didn't remember Doyle or his family at all — and asked to speak to Samuel's wife. The story Doyle gave her was that he'd been struck by Cecilia's postings and wanted to meet, in person, the woman who had so touched his life. After an extremely long vetting process, followed by an equally long recitation of rules of engagement for interacting with Cecilia, Glenda agreed to broach the subject of Doyle's coming for a visit the next time she saw Cecilia.

Several days passed, before Doyle received a phone call from a woman with a pleasant-sounding Southern accent.

"Doyle, this is your cousin Cecilia. Glenda informs me you'd like to come for a visit."

"That's right," Doyle said, somewhat surprised by the call. "I've been reading your posts, and they've really meant a lot to me."

"Well, you're a sweetheart for mentioning that," Cecilia said. "You're the first who's ever commented on them. I never know how my words are being received."

"They are very welcome in my home," Doyle said.

After a good deal of small talk, during which Cecilia laid out their entire genealogy and how they were related, she finally invited Doyle to join her one afternoon the following week. She gave him directions to her home, and told him how to knock when he arrived, so she'd know it was him.

On the appointed day, Doyle drove to Clayton, in the North Georgia mountains, and followed the directions to Cecilia's home, a split-level alpine style house that looked like it was built in the 50s. Following Cecilia's instructions, Doyle parked on the street in front of the house rather than the driveway, then went through the gate and up the walkway to the front porch. He rang the bell, gave three distinct knocks, then rang the bell again, which was the signal Cecilia had given him.

From inside, Doyle could hear a whirring, and a few moments later, the door opened, and Cecilia greeted him. Once he was inside, she locked both the screen door and the entry door, then boarded a nearby motorized scooter, and led Doyle into her home.

"Did you have any trouble finding me?" Cecilia said.

"Not at all," Doyle said. "I'm familiar with Clayton. It was just a matter of locating your street."

"That's good," she said.

The house was immaculately furnished, and seemed to Doyle well-preserved, as though he was visiting a museum rather than a residence. Doyle became aware of a cat mewing from somewhere in the house, and as they proceeded along, this became louder. Occasionally, Doyle would catch sight of other cats, cautiously regarding him from behind furniture, or from atop cabinets. Cecilia had always struck Doyle as one of those people who wouldn't be heard from for several weeks until her neighbors discovered her body, partially eaten by her cats.

They finally entered a sitting room near the rear of the house, where a calico sat by the window, sometime pacing and mewing.

"This is Dinky," Cecilia said. "She's been in here just talking to me all morning."

"What does she say?" Doyle asked.

Cecilia stared at him a long moment.

"I don't know. She's a cat. They don't speak English. I suppose she wants something to eat. That's usually why she makes a fuss." Shaking her finger at the cat, she finished, "But it's too early for her to eat yet and she knows it."

Cecilia stopped toward the middle of the sitting room and addressed Doyle. "I've taken the liberty of preparing a few snacks for us, so I hope you're hungry."

"I could go for a bite to eat," he replied. He was led into a dining room with a buffet setup that would rival a large hotel. Steamer trays of shrimp, beef kabobs, and chicken were set up, along with several types of cheese cut into bite sized cubes, a massive fruit salad, and several other delicacies. Doyle filled a couple of plates, then followed Cecilia back into her sitting room.

As they were eating, Doyle said, "As I've said, your posts have been very meaningful to me, but recently my hard drive crapped out and I lost the directory I was using to store them, and now the ones I saved are gone."

"Oh dear," Cecilia said. "No backup?"

"I hate to admit, I'm not very good at keeping backups of my files," Doyle said.

"Bless your heart," Cecilia said. She rolled away from him. "Well don't you worry. I keep copies of everything I send out."

"Oh, thank heavens," Doyle said. "It would be great to have a complete set again."

"I sure do," Cecilia said. "In fact, I have a bound copy which I'd be happy to let you have."

"You are amazing," Doyle said.

"Do you have any favorites?" she said from the other room.

"Please don't make me choose," Doyle said. "They all have special meaning for me."

A few hours later, Doyle left with several large containers of food, and a notebook filled with every note Cecilia had issued.

Five Points was where the city of Atlanta began with the convergence of five rail lines prior to the Civil War. This made it a bustling center for commerce, slowed only by the inconvenience of General Sherman's troops burning the city to the ground in 1864 from which the city quickly recovered. The MARTA station which derives its name from the area continues the tradition of being an important transportation hub for people around town. On Saturdays, it's not out of the ordinary to see speakers on makeshift stands, cajoling passersby to stop and listen.

Armed with Cecilia's epistles, Doyle targeted Five Points one Saturday afternoon, and he determined that the area around the station would be the ideal spot to start his project. Bowing to local standards, Doyle wore a G-string with sandals for his excursion. Upon arrival, he was glad to see there wasn't already a presentation going on, just a street preacher using a ventriloquist's dummy to mouth the words to a recorded sermon, who most were ignoring. Doyle found a location where he could be easily observed and heard, but which afforded him a quick getaway if things went awry. He opened the notebook Cecilia had given him, and in a clear, loud voice, began reciting the first of her posts.

> "Hear these words which originate from the Son; for those who hear are blest and curst. Seek to know that which is unknowable and let the darkness shine forth to enlighten. He that commands speaks disturbing words of comfort. Doubt not his wisdom or ignorance; reflect upon his symbols to guide. Cast no doubt upon the one who proclaims these truths, for it is the Son who gives authority and through him all will be enlightened.

> "For he is the light in the darkness and the darkness itself; he is the start of the journey and its destination; he commands all things and is ruled by them; his whispered words thunder throughout the cos-

mos. The Son was there when all began and will exist when all is gone; his countenance is hideous in its beauty and monstrous in its insignificance. He is strength and weakness; truth and falsehood; his glory is mediocrity and he speaks that which cannot be vocalized."

Those who bothered to take notice, couldn't figure out why a nearly naked white man was hanging around reading what sounded like nonsense to them, and most who stopped to listen were amused by the spectacle. It would be an interesting story to tell friends or relatives, they thought — more of the craziness inherent in being downtown. Some took him seriously, though.

The preacher with the ventriloquist's dummy stopped his recording and walked over holding the dummy to see what this new speaker was all about. People couldn't figure out whether to be amused or intrigued, and so, many were both. Sure, what he was saying was nonsense, but it was a special kind of nonsense, and every now and again, he'd say something that sounded vaguely religious which gave his words added weight. The people who carefully listened concluded such nonsense had not been uttered since the time of the prophets. They began paying attention.

Having concluded the first of his missives, Doyle started interpreting the words, and people really started to take notice. By the time he was on his third passage, the crowd had grown considerably. Then, just as mysteriously as he'd appeared, he closed the notebook and went on his way, leaving the bystanders clamoring for more.

He returned the following day, and a few folks had shown up, hoping to see him again. Within minutes, he had another large crowd, who hung on his every passage, some nodding, some clapping, but most just enrapt by his words, and the clear and concise way he delivered them. This was someone who deserved their attention.

Following several weekend excursions, Doyle became known as The Naked One, though Doyle identified himself as The Pastor. Each weekend, the crowds grew larger and more unwieldy, to the point that officials from the station suggested Doyle should relocate, so he told his followers to meet him in Woodruff Park a few blocks away, and from there, the crowds grew more and more. It was only a matter of time before the media took notice, and one afternoon, Doyle was gratified to see several news vans parked nearby, including the coveted one from Action News.

The Action News reporter approached him, asked him some questions about what he was doing and why, then taped him giving one of his sermons. For Doyle, it was the culmination of all his endeavors. Finally, he felt he was making a difference and he could see nothing but bigger and better things ahead for him.

On this same afternoon, it happened that Cecilia decided to take a break from her stenographic endeavors and decompress by watching some television. She rolled into the living room and tuned in Action News, only to be greeted by a disturbing sight. It was that man who had come to visit her, claiming to be her cousin, Doyle, only now he was almost totally naked, in a park in downtown Atlanta, reciting something. As she listened, she began to mouth the words he was speaking, and she realized they'd come from her. She wheeled her scooter over to her filing cabinet and opened the middle drawer. She removed a notebook and thumbed through it until she found the exact missive he was quoting.

"No!" she exclaimed. "Just no."

The reporter interviewing Doyle was inquiring about some sort of gathering he was having in Woodruff Park that evening, and Doyle talked about his congregation.

"You will not pervert the words of the Son," Cecilia said.

At that moment, a sort of energy overtook her, and she rose from her scooter. Her legs felt a bit wobbly at first, but as she moved, she became stronger and more sure-footed. She took down as much of the info as she could from the news report and began preparing herself to do what she had not done in more than ten years. She was going to have to leave her house. She had to put a stop to this sacrilege.

Going into her closet, she found the only dress clothing she had that still fit her properly was her tartan outfit from gatherings of Clan Baskin, so she took it out and started dressing. On her way to the garage, she grabbed her father's fez from the Shriners. She went through the kitchen into the garage and unlocked her car.

She hoped she could still remember how to drive, since she was certain her license had expired. Once she cranked the car, it all came back to her and she maneuvered out of the garage and onto the road. She followed the signs to the freeway and set her course for Atlanta.

That night, the crowd surrounding Doyle swelled to three times its normal size. Fueled by reports on several news agencies around town, people were anxious to hear this man who people were describing as a true prophet, one not seen since ancient times. Doyle tried to contain his enthusiasm, pretending to humbly stand by until the exact moment his talk was to begin, but he had convinced himself that this night would make or break his movement. At last, he headed to the speaker's stand and nodded to the crowd. He read through the first of Cecilia's missives, then began unraveling its mysteries for the assembly, who all fell silent to hear what he had to say.

Suddenly, from the back of the crowd the silence was shattered by a high and shrill voice, filled with rancor, "Charlatan! You're perverting the words of the Son."

A distinct gasp went through the crowd and everyone turned to see a short, squat woman, with dark, graying hair, wearing what appeared to be some sort of Scottish attire, with a Shriner's fez jauntily positioned on her head.

"You are committing a sacrilege," she went on, "and in the name of the Son, I command you to cease!"

The crowd parted as she moved toward the speaker's stand. Doyle could do nothing but stand there, transfixed, as if unable to process what he was seeing. The only word he could manage to utter was, "Cecilia?"

"This man is a fake," she proclaimed. "He has stolen the words of the Son, given solely to me, and perverted them for his own selfish purposes."

The crowd was perplexed. Who was this strange woman bedecked in tartan and a fez, and why was she saying such inflammatory things about The Pastor?

"Is it true?" someone from the crowd yelled. "Pastor, is she telling the truth?"

Doyle looked around at the crowd, which was now staring balefully at him. He shrugged.

"Well. Yes. She typed the stuff, that's true," Doyle said.

From there, pandemonium broke out, with equal parts of the crowd pushing forward to be closer to this amazing woman, with some loudly declaring The Pastor to be a fraud. People were turning left and right, screaming at anyone who happened to be within earshot of them, flailing hands, some fainting, others standing around, totally befuddled by this sudden turn of events. In the midst of all this, Cecilia made it to the speaker's stand, where she began reciting one of her epistles from memory.

"She's not reading it," someone remarked. "It is her!"

The crowd went wild, cheering, hooting and hollering, waving their hands around like they were in church, and for many of them, that's exactly where they were. Here was the true message, delivered by the person who knew it best, and everyone was enraptured.

"She's the voice — the conduit," one of the crowd cried out.

Since no one seemed to be paying close attention to him, Doyle took this opportunity to saunter quietly away, and once he was a few hundred yards from the melee, he took off running as he'd never run before. He had a little trouble hailing a cab at Peachtree and Baker Street, mainly due to the fact that he was hardly wearing any clothes, but once one stopped for him and he convinced the driver he could pay the fare, he asked to be taken to his condo in Doraville. There, he unplugged his phone, packed a suitcase, and put on some shorts, a polo shirt, and sneakers, then hopped in his car and headed North on I-85. He had no idea where he was headed, he just knew it wasn't a great idea to stay in Atlanta right then. He would eventually find a job in Research Triangle Park, after having grown a bushy beard, and using his first name, Richard.

The movement Doyle initiated with the purloined writing has continued into the current day, now headed by the Prophetess Cecilia, who never again retreated to the seclusion of her home. Some years ago, parishioners pooled their money to purchase a three-story house on Moreland Avenue, near Freedom Parkway, to ground their church to a specific location. Each day, the Prophetess spends several hours receiving the words from above, before descending to her followers to deliver the morning's message, then heads into the kitchen to oversee preparation of that day's menu. Most in the neighborhood regard them as kooks, but generally harmless, and their outreach program, in particular, their daily communal meals, which are freely shared with any of the local residents, or anyone else who happens by, are the envy of all who partake.

Atomic Punk

Roscoe Delahunt is a troll; there seems little doubt of that. For years, he has surfed the Internet, looking to rain on someone's parade, and has rarely lacked people to torment. In the heady days before the World Wide Web, when Usenet was the primary vehicle for Internet discourse, Roscoe, known as "Scoey" to his fellow undergraduates at Case Western Reserve University in Cleveland, established himself as the supreme flame lord, cross-posting much off-topic drivel to numerous inappropriate news groups. When the earliest social media platform, MySpace, began in the early aughts, Scoey shifted gears and considered himself a pioneer in an emerging area of communication, anti-social media.

Once college ended, Scoey headed to Atlanta, where the post-Olympic tech boom was well under way. He found employment working as a user support specialist with Cairo Enterprises (which Scoey quickly learned was pronounced Kay-ro), an Internet startup headed by David Cairo, an Atlanta native who founded it as a web development company and took it public in 1997. Following the initial public offering, the company diversified to such an extent that it was no longer clear exactly what it did, other than generate headlines. Roscoe was sensible enough to sign up for the company's profit-sharing opportunities, so when the IPO happened, he received a few hundred shares that added up to quite a bit of money, enough to allow him to become an independent contractor, where he could charge more for essentially the same work.

On Usenet in the 90s, Scoey was known as Atomic Punk, which is now the name of his blog, where he rails against "all the things stupid people do that piss me off." In addition to an extensive list of grievances, Scoey has over four thousand readers, who hang on his every word. No topic is off-limits to "The Punk" and he gladly skewers religion, politics, music, films, television, and the cult of celebrity, posting anywhere from a few terse lines, to several hundred words about once every four to six hours, around the clock. Whenever Scoey's away on vacation, he sometimes lets his cranky seventy-year-old neighbor post in his stead, and his readers are often perplexed by the sudden shift in focus from insightful commentary on contemporary society, to complaining about the senior discount at Denny's, and "those damn Brewster boys upstairs". Diehard fans of The Punk enjoy these interludes, viewing them as evidence of his utter contempt for even his closest fans, whereas more casual readers simply skim the blog until the regular posts resume.

Scoey is as inconspicuous in real-life as he is infamous online. Somewhat short, very overweight, with thick glasses, prematurely balding, and clothes that look like he slept in them the night before (oftentimes because he has) Scoey looks like someone who probably shouldn't be left alone with children. He currently handles technical support for the software development division of Bickering Plummet, working from home, walking technologically-challenged people through installing software, or trouble shooting hardware problems, on systems way more advanced than their level of technical knowledge warrants. His experience with clients does little to elevate his opinion of the human race. On the phone, however, he's a comforting presence, his melodious baritone soothing frazzled nerves as he endures numerous apologies for "wasting your time" and generally making life slightly more bearable for people totally befuddled by the modern computing landscape. When he's not on the phone with a client, or jotting a few lines for his blog, Scoey spends his time surfing cable television for stories about sharks.

Despite his socially unacceptable appearance, and enduring disgust for almost everyone he knows, Scoey does have a girlfriend, Aileen Bevels, who he's been seeing for about four years, after meeting her at Dragon Con. Aileen is above average in height and exceptionally skinny, which Scoey would worry about if he hadn't seen her at Steak & Shake, putting away several burgers, with fries, and a large shake, then ordering a Takhomasak. Once, she told him that she has a very high metabolism and needs to eat to keep from losing weight, and that, at the doctor, she never registers a blood pressure. She always has a slightly garlicky scent to her, even after showering or when wearing perfume.

When Scoey and Aileen were first talking about getting married, she wanted to sit down with him and disclose all their previous sexual encounters — she had a detailed list — but Scoey strenuously objected. Instead, he told her they should just go to the doctor and get some tests done, and if everything checked out okay, they could proceed from there. In fact, Scoey hasn't had nearly as many previous relationships as Aileen claims she's had, and he really doesn't want her to know, nor does he wish to hear her wax nostalgic about some guy she met in a bar in junior college. Despite the discussions, neither seems in much of a hurry to settle down, which suits Scoey, who's not sure he wants someone to have unlimited access to his private life. He doesn't really have much to hide, and that's what worries him the most.

Tonight, he's at the club where Aileen works as a server, meeting with Rebecca Asher, a local reporter and fellow blogger, as well as a mutual friend of him and Aileen. Scoey sometimes takes on research assignments as a side job, and Rebecca asked Scoey to find information on someone. Scoey met Rebecca at a fantasy con after she'd spent much of the evening trying to pick up Aileen, who'd gone in a costume patterned after Camilla from *The Vampire Lovers*. Scoey relished the prospect of watching Aileen and Rebecca in bed together, but Aileen dashed both their hopes by stating that, "I don't swing that way, darlin'. Not even for you." Speaking to her in the wake of this crushing disappointment, Scoey came to realize Rebecca shared the same level of disillusionment with people as him, and he spent the rest of the night comparing notes with her. The evening ended with Scoey and Aileen practically carrying Rebecca to their hotel suite, where they let her crash on the couch, since she was obviously too drunk to drive.

Rebecca is an inch or two shorter than Scoey, with dark, curly hair that's long and which she rarely pulls back. She's almost always decked out in cargo shorts, high-top sneakers or loafers without socks, with a polo shirt or a buttoned-down oxford with the sleeves rolled up. Today, she's wearing an Atlanta Braves jersey with the number ten on it — Chipper Jones's number — which is at least a size too big for her. Scoey has noted that Rebecca always has a "lived-in" look about her, as though she's used to sleeping in her car or on other people's couches.

"I'm sure you're aware, the woman you asked me to investigate is one of the hottest sound engineers in town," Scoey says, "CC Belmonte. Her bio says she's worked with artists as diverse as Usher and the Indigo Girls."

"I know her as a sound tech and deejay at several clubs," Rebecca says. "She also works with that brother and sister group, Echo."

"Yeah, she's their exclusive sound engineer," he says. "Been with them since they started in the business."

"That's where I first caught site of her, working the boards for them at Blind Willie's," she says. "What have you managed to dig up on her?"

"For one thing, she hates having her photo taken," Scoey says. "No one I spoke to has ever seen one of her as an adult."

"Is that why Echo allows fans to record their shows, but not their setup?"

"Probably," Scoey says. "She's very enigmatic. Her bio is never more than a line or two. No birthplace, no education, just lists the artists she's worked with, but that's common."

"Come on, Scoey, I'm paying for info I can't find at clubs or recording companies. I know how to search them."

"Now, don't fret," he says. "I'm worth my weight in gold. I got on LexisNexis and ran the name and came across some interesting info. She's apparently been on her own since high school. Belmonte isn't the name she was born with."

"Don't tell me she's married," Rebecca says, covering her face and concluding with a groan.

"She's not," he says. "Looks like she may have changed her name."

"From what?"

"Unfortunately, it was in the eighties," Scoey says. "Superior court records from that time haven't been digitized. I tried running a search on the AJC archives, since she'd have had to publish the info, but their issues from then aren't on the web either."

"So, you bring me nothing," Rebecca says.

"Do you honestly think I left it at that, oh ye of little faith?" Scoey tells her. "This gave me very important info on where and when to look. Records not found on the Internet are on microfilm at the courthouse or archives."

"Did you?" she says.

He retrieves an envelope from his jacket pocket. "Of course. You're paying me for info and info I deliver." He hands the envelope to Rebecca. "She changed her name in '89 in DeKalb. Before that, she seems to have been declared an emancipated minor in Middle Georgia. I couldn't get much on that, because it was a juvenile court case and the records are sealed."

"You are the man," Rebecca says and hands him a bank deposit envelope with cash in it.

"Always a pleasure," he says, placing the envelope in his coat pocket. "What are you going to do with the info?"

"I haven't decided yet," Rebecca says. "This woman intrigues the hell out of me, though. She's like the Sphinx."

"I thought you said she's an Amazon."

"An Amazonian Sphinx, then," Rebecca says. "Say, listen, I've got another job for you." She removes a VHS tape from her bag and hands it to him. The video case identifies it as a porno film from the 70s or 80s. Scoey looks it over.

"Hot LA Nights?" he says. "Doesn't seem to be quite your speed."

"One of my friends had it at a party," she says. "There's an actress I want you to check out. In the credits, she's listed as Carmen Delectable."

"Hmm, find an obscure actress from the 70s, in a profession where no one uses real names," he says. "Someone who might very well have died in the AIDS epidemic."

"Oh no," Rebecca says. "She's very much alive and well in Atlanta."

"I'll do what I can," Scoey says.

Rebecca slides to the edge of her seat and stands. "Great. I'll be in touch."

Scoey was never much of an outright hacker in school, focusing more on the social engineering aspects than cracking. He'd learned all the nuances of finessing a password out of a harried office temp or general secretary or coaxing the name or email of an executive at a given company from some random drone who happened to be in his or her cubicle when Scoey was making cold calls. He now finds these skills helpful in his job in tech support, as he often has to wring details of a problem out of folks with no computer savvy at all. His main talent is in knowing where to look for information, and he's cultivated a variety of online and other resources which help him when he needs to research an issue.

The video Rebecca has given him piques his interest, particularly since she suggested she knows the actress and that she's in the Atlanta area. Scoey wonders about Rebecca's motives in searching for this person, since she'd be considerably older than Rebecca, probably the age of Rebecca's parents. Why does Rebecca want to identify her?

As it turns out, researching obscure performers from 70s and 80s era porno movies is right up Scoey's alley, as he considers himself an expert in adult films from this time period. Scoey's first experience of "adult" videos was the amateurish Gonzo porn distributed on the Internet in the 90s; for him the 70s, into the early 80s was the "golden era" of pornography in the United States. Budgets were big, the writing was often above par, especially on films produced on the East Coast, and the actors and actresses sometimes had a modicum of acting talent. Many of the filmmakers of the era, such as the Mitchell Brothers, took the genre seriously, and produced work that sometimes rivaled the product coming out of legitimate Hollywood studios. Scoey prefers East

Coast studios, who put more into production, even if the actors weren't as hot, to the West Coast, who had hotter stars, but the storylines were less important, though he prefers the products from either coast in that era to the dreck which followed in the wake of the "digital revolution" of the late 90s into the early 00s. With any sort of fantasy genre, Scoey finds it's the storylines and not the action itself that stimulates his interest. Otherwise, the action becomes mechanical, divorced from context, and Scoey finds he really needs the context.

He pops the video into a VCR he has hooked up to his computer and digitizes the entire film, then makes snippets of video that feature the particular actress. What first catches his eye about her, is how young she seems. It's apparent she's no older than her late-teens to early-twenties, which is fairly common in that business. She's very attractive, with a clean-cut, girl-next-door appearance, despite the fact she's wearing wigs and tons of makeup. One feature that catches his eye is a tattoo of an ornate heart on her left shoulder, which appears to be split in half. He notes another actress in the film, billed as Tiffany Sweetness, with a similar tattoo. Carmen's tattoo is of the left side of the heart and Tiffany's is of the right side.

Scoey is aware that many actresses in hetero porn are lesbian or bisexual.

He hops onto the Internet and uploads the clips to a private message board for other fans of the pornography of that era. Along with it, he types a note:

"Who can give me the low down on the hottie in this clip? She's credited as Carmen Delectable."

Within an hour, others on the board have responded with about fifteen to twenty titles of films she appeared in. Some have included clips of her performing. It's definitely the same woman.

"She wasn't in the business long, apparently," one respondent says. "Such a shame. She's a stone fox."

"She's always in films with Tiffany Sweetness," another says. "Some of the skin mags from the time hint that they were an item."

One of the moderators for the board sends Scoey a private message.

"I knew her when I was the lighting tech for films around that time. She was only in the biz for about four years, and not very active. Last time I heard from her, she was a nurse in LA, but that was in the 90s."

"Any chance you can share her true ID?" Scoey says.

"Why do you want it?"

"Actually, I'm researching this for a friend," Scoey types. "Not sure why she wants the info."

"I have to respect her privacy," the moderator says. "But she used to work with an anti-exploitation group that helps girls get out of prostitution and porno. Journey from Darkness, I think."

"Any truth to the rumors on her and Tiffany Sweetness?" Scoey says.

"They were a couple," the moderator says, "but Tiffany died from AIDS complications around 1990. Carmen took it very hard. Look, Carmen is a decent person who's been through some tough times. I'd examine very closely the motives of whoever's asking about her."

"Will do," Scoey types. "Thanks for the info."

Watching the clips again, and hearing the moderator's words echo in his mind, Scoey has an intuition and picks up the phone to call Aileen.

"Hey, sweetie, who's that person Becky's always complaining about?"

"You'll have to narrow that down some, hon," Aileen says. "Becky complains about a lot of people."

"I'm not talking simply griping. This person always gets an extra dose of vitriol."

"Oh yeah, her aunt," Aileen says. "Rochelle, or something similar."

"Rachel," Scoey says. "Thanks, sweetie."

Scoey searches on LexisNexis for Rebecca's name, and he finds an obituary for Sharon Asher which lists Rebecca, her brother, Steven, and Sharon's sister, Rachel Lawson. Scoey does a search for Rachel. Her name appears in reference to the staff at St. Joseph's Hospital in Atlanta, as a nurse, and as a contact for an organization called Journey From Night, which states that it helps exploited women leave the sex industry. He notes an upcoming conference at a nearby church and decides to ask Aileen to check it out. There's a photo of Rachel at Journey From Night; Scoey examines it closely. He saves it to his computer and calls up a screen shot he made of the actress Carmen Delectable for comparison and tries to imagine her twenty years older. He notes similarities but can't decide.

Aileen enters the fellowship hall of the Unitarian church on

Cliff Valley Way and stops at the reception table to sign in and pick up a name tag. She's attending a conference on exploited women at Roscoe's instigation, and she's been assigned to locate a specific person, Rachel Lawson, Rebecca's aunt. He hasn't said why he needs her to engage Rachel, just that she's to make contact if possible and provide him with her impression of the encounter.

Aileen is an aspiring actress, and enjoys meeting people, so she gladly took the assignment. Scoey has showed her an older photo of Rachel, and Aileen hasn't been in the hall for very long, before she spots a dark-haired, very attractive woman who appears to be in her forties, wearing a light top with spaghetti straps. She's talking to some young women, but as Aileen approaches, the women depart, and the woman looks toward Aileen and glances at her name tag.

"Hi Aileen, I'm Rachel," she says, extending her hand. Aileen shakes it. "What can I tell you about Journey From Night?"

"I don't have specific questions," Aileen says, "except how to get involved. I think the work you're doing is phenomenal."

"Let me get you one of our brochures," Rachel says. She pivots to her right to pick up the brochure, and as she does, Aileen catches sight of a tattoo on Rachel's shoulder, the left half of an ornate heart.

"Nice ink," Aileen says. "Local artist?"

"Oh, no," Rachel says, touching her left shoulder. "I got it in LA in the 70s."

"Who wears the other half?" Aileen says.

Rachel gives her a warm smile. "Someone who's no longer with us."

"I'm sorry," Aileen says. "I didn't mean to bring up a sad memory."

"Not at all," Rachel says. "I have very wonderful memories of her, even though I miss her every day."

Aileen takes the brochure and moves to another table. Later, there's a presentation; Rachel speaks on behalf of Journey From Night, giving a detailed history of how she became involved with the sex industry in Los Angeles in the 70s and 80s, and how it cost her someone she loved dearly. Listening to her, Aileen is impressed by how open and honest Rachel is about her past.

Her report back to Scoey is very complimentary of Rachel and how impressive Aileen found her to be. She shows him the brochure and tells him of their conversation about the tattoo.

"I don't know why Becky always complains so much about her

aunt," Aileen says. "She seems like just the sort of person Becky needs to listen to."

Scoey still won't share the reason why he sent her there, and she knows enough not to press him. Aileen tells him she's thinking of volunteering with Journey From Night and he encourages her.

"I found the info you wanted," Scoey tells Rebecca when they meet again. "She was an actress in the 70s and early-80s. Starred in about twenty or so movies. Never a featured performer, almost always way down in the billing."

He hands her the envelope and she takes out her payment.

"Any chance I can get my hands on more of her movies?"

"A couple of these have some pretty big names in them, so they should be available," he says.

Aileen comes over and joins them. "Hey Becky." She sits beside Roscoe and kisses his cheek. "Transacting business?"

"Yeah, giving Becky the lowdown on that individual you scouted," he says.

"Why do you want this info?" Aileen asks.

"I'm planning a surprise for a friend," Rebecca says.

"A friend?" Aileen says. "This is your aunt, isn't it? Rachel Lawson."

"Yeah, it's her," Rebecca replies. "The bitch has locked me out of the house and won't let me see Stevie. I'm taking her to court to become Stevie's guardian."

"How does this info factor into that?" Aileen says, looking between Rebecca and Roscoe.

Rebecca waves the envelope. "Once they see the films she was in, they'll realize the kind of slut she is and give me custody in a heartbeat."

"This is the information you dug up for her?" Aileen says.

"It's public information," Roscoe says. "She could have looked it up for herself."

"Then why didn't she?" Aileen says, now staring at Rebecca.

"What difference does it make?" Rebecca says.

"Have you even talked to your aunt about any of this?" Aileen says. "She's pretty open about it."

"You met her?" Rebecca says.

"Yes. I was very impressed. She's a great lady. About the only person who can't see that is you."

"I'm not paying for a character reference," she says. "I need dirt to spread around about this bitch."

"Your aunt is a good woman who made a few mistakes when she was younger," Aileen says, "and you're going to crucify her in court for that? You call yourself a feminist?"

"Oh, excuse me," Rebecca says. "I wasn't aware I needed to justify my actions to my server."

"You don't want to travel down this road," Roscoe says, covering his face.

"I'm just your server, am I?" Aileen says. "Well then check out the sign by the register. We have the right to refuse service to anyone for any reason. Now, are you going to leave quietly, or do I need to get the manager?"

"Get serious," Rebecca says.

Aileen stands. "I've never been more serious in my life. We're done, Becky. Don't come in here and don't call Scoey for anymore projects, if this is how you're going to use the research he gives you."

Rebecca looks at Roscoe who shakes his head. "Don't look at me. You heard what she said."

She grabs her bag and gets up. "Fine." She throws some money on the table for her drinks and leaves.

"I'm serious about this, Scoey," Aileen says. "I don't want you having anything more to do with her."

"Not a problem," he says.

After Aileen severs ties with Rebecca, the only way Roscoe is able to keep up with her, is via her blog, The Frantic Feminist, where she publishes rants, social commentary, movie and music reviews, or through her work with Creative Loafing.

A few months after their last encounter with Rebecca, Aileen convinces Scoey to find a place together, and a realtor finds them a good deal on a fixer-upper in East Atlanta. It's here that an associate of David Cairo finds him early in 2004 with a proposal for work on a contract for the NSA, which promises to keep Roscoe busy for the next several years.

One morning in early-December 2005, Scoey and Aileen are at home when she answers the phone, then turns to him.

"It's Rachel Lawson," Aileen says. "Wonder why she's calling you."

"Only one way to find out," he says as he takes the phone. "Roscoe here. Yes, Ms. Lawson, what can I do for you? Yes. We were friends and I did some research on a few stories for Becky a couple of years ago." His expression changes to shock. "Oh my god. When did this happen? Thank you for letting me know. I'm sorry for your loss. You, too."

He puts down the phone and won't face Aileen. She goes to him. "What is it?"

"Becky's dead."

"No," Aileen says, putting her hands over her mouth. "What happened?"

"Car accident outside Braselton," he says. "She was coming back from some film festival. Rachel didn't give me many details."

He turns to Aileen, who's crying, and wraps his arms around her. They comfort one another for several minutes. Still holding Aileen, Scoey says, "This is probably a really weird time to bring this up, but let's get married."

Aileen pulls back to look at him. "You're right. This is a really weird time to bring it up."

"Look, we can debate the merits and question the timing all we want, and, yes, we're pretty much married already, but life's short, sweetie. This just proves it. I don't want to spend another week without you as my wife."

In response, Aileen kisses and embraces him. "Let's do this."

Phoenix

Yea, though I walk through the valley of the shadow of death, I will fear no evil: for thou art with me... Psalm 23:4 (KJV)

First Christine

The Curse of Zachariah Messner

Zachariah Messner was a stern and pious man, a deacon at the Messianic Holiness Congregation, a small church in Houston County, Georgia, which had no affiliation to any of the recognized Christian denominations. A man with few pleasures in life, he believed himself to be head of his household: he insisted his wife arise at least a half hour before him to start breakfast and would not allow a morsel to be consumed before the morning prayer was said. He started and ended each day with a reading of the Bible and was always mindful of how those around him perceived his and his family's actions. Those who knew him often commented on his steadfastness and piety. He clung to his beliefs, not because he felt them in his heart, but because they made the world manageable for him.

In this same congregation, was another deacon, James Frederick, and there was no one more different than Messner. Frederick was a jovial man, who enjoyed the presence of others and made those with whom he interacted feel comfortable and more certain in their beliefs. While Messner was rigid and unyielding in his faith, Frederick recognized the subtle shades of gray that existed in all interactions. One could claim that Frederick's motto was "always forgive" while Messner's was "never forget". Needless to say, the two were frequently at odds over church doctrine, with Frederick an unapologetic believer in the Apostle Paul's message of love and fellowship, while Messner called for a rigid "Old Testament" adherence to scripture.

When he was in his thirties, Messner met and married Mylene Tucker, an attractive woman, twelve years his junior, with a good heart and a pleasant disposition which contrasted sharply with that of her husband. Despite this, their marriage seemed happy as they anticipated starting a family.

Within a few months, Mylene learned she was pregnant, but less than two months in, she miscarried. Nevertheless, the couple persisted and six months after her first conception, Mylene was expecting another.

This one, too, ended abruptly, establishing a pattern that would recur again and again.

As it became a predictable occurrence, Messner took to blaming Mylene, attributing her inability to carry a child on some moral failing he had yet to ascertain. Her once cheery disposition withered, as Zachariah found more and more ways in which she failed in her devotion.

The end came in the ninth year of their marriage. Zachariah arrived home one evening and found Mylene dead in the bathtub having cut her wrist using one of his straight razors. On the mirror he found the words, "Into thy hands I commend my spirit."

Messner wasn't long in finding another wife and less than four months after burying Mylene, he married Selma, the thirty-one-year-old spinster sister of Alvin Porter.

Theirs wasn't a particularly loving marriage. Changing wives had not changed Messner's fortunes in starting a family. Just as Mylene before her, Selma endured numerous difficult pregnancies, which all ended within the first two to three months. Rather than look inward and wonder if, perhaps, he was the cause, Messner instead blamed Selma's lack of devotion on their misfortunes. As a result, Selma became despondent, and finally sought out Deacon Frederick for advice and counsel. He invited her to his home, so he could counsel her in private.

After this had gone on two or three times a week for nearly a month, Selma once again found she was pregnant. When she made it past four months, Messner's spirits were raised, and when Selma made it to term, Zachariah was certain the Lord had finally given him the son he hoped to mold into the perfect Christian warrior.

At last, Selma announced the time was at hand and Messner drove her to the regional medical center, where he waited in the maternity ward for news. Finally, a nurse emerged and called his name.

"Congratulations, Mr. Messner. You have a daughter."

"A girl," Zachariah said with little enthusiasm.

"That's right."

Zachariah took in the news, shook his head and walked out of the hospital.

Selma named the girl Christine.

Christine was a large baby, nearly ten pounds, and Selma was in labor with her for twenty-seven hours. Selma was in quite a bit of distress throughout since Zachariah forbade her from accepting anything for the pain, owing to Genesis 3:16 (KJV):

> "...in sorrow thou shalt bring forth children; and thy desire shall be to thy husband, and he shall rule over thee..."

While the doctors had not known the gender, based on how much weight Selma had gained, she and Zachariah assumed the child would be a boy. When she learned she had a girl and Zachariah had left the hospital, Selma took this as a bad sign. She wondered if, perhaps, her husband had done the math, or if, maybe the news that his new child wasn't the son he had prayed for so vigorously throughout her pregnancy was too much for Messner to bear. In any event, his lack of enthusiasm signaled to Selma that the worst was still to come.

Zachariah made it clear to Selma that caring for the baby did not take priority over her responsibilities as a wife, so, often, Christine was neglected as Selma saw to the needs of her husband. Despite this, Christine thrived, always large for her age. Doctors who examined her thought she was several months older than she actually was, and sometimes insisted on seeing her birth certificate to confirm. As she grew, she would often spend time with her uncle Alvin's family in another county, and, as Christine gained awareness of her situation, she was thankful for the warm and loving environment her uncle provided, versus the cold and rigid confines of her father's house. Alvin sometimes mentioned that he and his family would be happy to let Christine stay with them on a permanent basis, but Zachariah always said no.

"The girl's my responsibility," he'd say. Alvin decided it wasn't his place to tell another man how to raise his child.

One person who took a lot of interest in Christine was Deacon Frederick, and she always found him to be warm and accepting of her. He gave her peppermint candy and seemed to take a genuine delight in whatever she reported to him. His actions made Christine wish that Deacon Frederick was her father and that she could go live in his fine house in town, rather than the modest and unadorned household her mother maintained at Zachariah's insistence. Christine sometimes heard Frederick scold Messner for not showing her more affection.

"You got you a fine little girl there, Zachariah. You ought to treat her with more concern than you do."

"The Lord has given me this burden to endure and I shall endure it as I see fit," was Messner's reply.

Once, when Christine heard Frederick raise the issue with her mother, Selma replied, "He's my husband. I must yield to his judgment."

At age thirteen, Christine was considered awkward and pudgy, with full, rosy cheeks, very long feet and short, dark hair. Zachariah rarely spent any money on her, other than for food and what he paid for upkeep on their house. He especially didn't want to waste funds on clothes she'd only outgrow in less than a year, so her clothing was a hodgepodge of hand-me-downs from kindly neighbors with older kids, or tidbits Selma picked up at the local thrift shop for less than a dollar. The kids at school often teased her about her clothing, but despite this, Christine remained outwardly cheerful and friendly, often laughing along with the other kids, though sometimes when she was alone, she'd cry because of their taunting. Her best friend was Jodie Newcombe, and Christine spent her afternoons at Jodie's home, studying and doing their homework, since Zachariah forbade her from reading anything other than the Bible under his roof.

In school, Christine was mostly studious and polite, but in one class, English, she cracked jokes and talked during the lessons, prompting her teacher, Mr. Standridge, to keep her after school. When Christine was in detention, she never acted out, but was always polite and courteous.

"Is it okay if I read, Mr. Standridge?" Christine asked the first time she showed up after school.

"You may work on your assignments, Christine," he replied. "That's fine."

"No. I was hoping I could read some of those books over there," she said, pointing to the literary works he assigned to the older students.

"If you'd like," he said.

For the next few days, Christine reported for detention, and sat, quietly reading books from the shelf. The rate at which she finished them astonished Mr. Standridge and one afternoon, he asked her, "Why do you always act up in my class, Christine? I've spoken to your other teachers and they say you're a model student. Why are you disruptive in my class?"

Christine lowered her head. "I don't mean no disrespect, Mr. Standridge. I just wanted to read some of your books and figured if you kept me after class, I could."

"If you like to read, I can loan you the books."

"No sir. My father don't want me reading at the house."

"You can't read at home?"

"No sir. My father only lets me read the Bible at home. I have to leave my book bag at my friend Jodie's at night."

"I'll tell you what, Christine," Standridge said, "you can come here in the afternoon and read all you want. Tell your parents whatever you need to as to why you stayed after school. I won't count it against you."

"Thank you, Mr. Standridge," Christine said, very excited.

From then on, Christine was a regular presence in Mr. Standridge's classroom after school. While she normally would greet him when she entered, read for a while, then say goodbye as she exited, sometimes they'd have brief conversations.

"Is that your family?" Christine asked about a photo on his desk.

"It is. My mom and dad, brother Rex, and sister Claire."

"You still close with your sister?"

"I was. She died when we were children," he said.

"I'm so sorry to hear that," Christine said. "Was she in an accident or something?"

"No, she had a rare heart condition. Now they have a surgery that might have saved her, but they hadn't developed it back then. Such a shame."

"Bet you miss her."

"I do, Christine. Very much."

"Why ain't you married, Mr. Standridge?" Christine asked.

"Aren't, Christine. The proper way to say that is, 'Why aren't you married'."

Christine laughed. "Okay, Mr. Standridge. Why aren't you married? I mean, you're a good-looking guy. Lot of the older girls got crushes on you."

"Yes, I'm aware of that."

"You don't have to tell me if you don't want to," she said. "I'm just wondering."

"Not every man is marriage material Christine. I'm still young, though, so, who knows?"

As the school year progressed and the days grew shorter, Christine's visits in the afternoon became less frequent and when she was there, she hardly read anything before excusing herself to head to her friend's house. When Standridge asked her about it, she told him, "My parents expect me to be in before it gets dark. I need to get over to Jodie's house, so I can get my studying done."

"Surely your parents understand," Standridge said to her. "It's not your fault the seasons change."

"Not my father," she said, a note of fear evident in her voice. "He don't like it when I defy his words. No telling how he might react."

"Does he ever hit you, Christine?" Standridge said.

"Mostly it's Mama who gives me a whipping, usually because Daddy tells her to," she says. "Daddy says children are to be seen and not heard."

"Have they always been like this?" Standridge says.

"Long as I can remember."

"That's fine. You run along, Christine. I don't want you to get in trouble."

A few days later, Jodie tells Christine that Standridge asked some questions about her.

"What kind of questions?" Christine asked.

"He wanted to know if I'd been to your house," Jodie said.

"Why would he want to know that?"

"He just said he thought it was strange your father wouldn't let you read books there," Jodie said.

"Oh. Yeah. I told him that." Christine considered this. "He hasn't said nothing to me about it since then."

That Sunday, Christine was surprised when Mr. Standridge showed up at the Messianic Holiness Congregation. He arrived just before the service began and sat in the back. When Christine saw him, she smiled and waved. Her father took note of this and gave Standridge a long, cold stare. After the service, the Messners seemed anxious to leave, but Christine went over and said, "Hey Mr. Standridge. What you doing here?"

"I thought I'd check out a new congregation," he said. "The church I've been attending is in Macon and it's quite a drive first thing on Sunday."

Standridge looked at Zachariah and Selma, as though waiting for them to speak to him, and when neither did, he offered his hand to Zachariah and said, "Hello, I'm Lawrence Standridge, one of Christine's teachers."

Messner shook Standridge's hand, saying, "Pleased to meet you.

This is my wife, Selma."

Selma nodded to him without changing her facial expression or offering her hand. An awkward pause followed.

"Christine's a very good student," Standridge said. "I'm sure you're both very proud of her."

"Pride is a sin, Mr. Standridge," Messner said. "We do not yield to such temptations in my house."

With that, Messner indicated they needed to go.

"See you in school, Mr. Standridge," Christine said as they left.

Standridge was concerned about Christine's well-being, but wasn't sure how he could definitively prove wrongdoing on the part of her parents. He stopped in to see the school counselor.

"Have you ever talked to Christine Messner?"

"She's not been in," the counselor said. "From what I hear, she's above average. Nothing special, but she's never given us reason for concern."

"I'm worried her parents may be abusing her."

"What makes you think that?"

"She's seems to be afraid to defy her father," Standridge said.

"That could describe just about every student at this school," the counselor said. "People are pretty old fashioned around here."

"It's just a feeling I get," Standridge said.

"You'll need more than a feeling if you're going to accuse someone of child abuse," the counselor said. "Have you seen any marks? Bruises?"

"No. Nothing like that."

"Then you need to be really careful. A family can be torn apart by accusations like that."

"Isn't there someone who can look into it?" Standridge said.

"DFACS, but they're going to want more proof than how you feel."

Wanting to gather more information, Standridge would casually bring up Christine's name when talking to another of her teachers. They all considered her to be a bright student who was very polite but who didn't stand out in class. He learned that the Messners never attended parent/teacher events at the school and had never had a conference with any of their daughter's instructors. Standridge used this as a pretense to visit the family's home.

He eschewed his usual afternoon time to grade papers, since he knew Christine usually went to her friend Jodie's after school and he wanted to speak to her mother alone. When he knocked on the door at the Messner's, he heard movement from inside, and a moment later, a curtain was pulled open, and he saw Selma peering out at him. He waved and said, "Afternoon Mrs. Messner. May I speak with you?"

It took another minute for Selma to open the door a crack and look out at him.

"What you want?" she said.

"May I come in?"

"I reckon it's better for you to stay outside," she said. "My husband's not home."

"I wanted to talk to you about Christine," he said. "I noted you've never been to the school for a conference, so I wanted to check and see if you had any concerns or questions about her classes or grades."

"I ain't been there because I don't care about her grades," she said. "School board says we got to send her to classes, so we do."

"As I said when we spoke at church, she's a very bright young woman," he told her. "But she doesn't always apply herself."

"Look, you want to talk, you need to come back when my husband's here," she said. "I got things I need to get done. Ain't got time to waste on unimportant stuff."

With that, she closed the door.

Lawrence leaned in and said in a raised voice, "Your daughter's education isn't unimportant."

The following Friday, Lawrence was in his classroom after school, when Zachariah Messner paid him a visit.

"Selma says you were by the house the other day," Messner said.

"That's right. I stopped in to talk about Christine."

"You are not to visit my house again when I am away," Messner said. "If you wish to have a meeting, you need to call first and make sure I'm there."

"I'm very concerned about your daughter, Mr. Messner," Standridge said.

"You needn't concern yourself with the girl," Messner said. "My wife and I know what's best for her."

"She says you won't let her read at home," Standridge said.

"She has her mind filled with worldly affairs all day at this school," Messner replied. "I won't permit it under my roof."

"My roof. My house. Why is it you never say, 'our house'?"

"The scriptures say the man is lord of his home and family," Messner said. "I provide for their welfare."

"I strongly suspect you're abusing your daughter, Mr. Messner," Standridge said. "I just can't prove it — yet."

"How I choose to raise that girl is no concern of yours," Messner said. "You'd do well to look to your own affairs, and not be so worried about other people's private business."

"What does that mean?" Standridge said.

"You're not married, are you?" Messner said. "A lot of people might find that rather odd."

"My marital status isn't relevant to this conversation, sir," Standridge said.

"We'll see," Messner said, then turned and left.

The following Monday, Christine was not in school. Halfway through the day, before the start of Standridge's first afternoon class, the principal showed up in his classroom with another instructor.

"Lawrence, would you come with me please?" the principal said.

"I'm about to start class, Joe," Standridge said. "What's this about?"

"Tom here is going to take over your remaining classes," the principal said. "We have a rather grave situation and we need you to help us sort it out."

Standridge accompanied the principal to the office, where the sheriff was waiting.

"What's going on here?" Standridge said.

The principal closed and locked the door. He nodded to the sheriff.

"Mr. Standridge, a parent in this school came to my office this morning with some very serious allegations against you," the sheriff said.

"Allegations?" Standridge said. "What sort of allegations?"

"Selma Messner has accused you of molesting her daughter, Christine."

"What? That's ridiculous," Standridge said. "I haven't touched Christine. Where would she get a crazy idea like that?"

"She says that Christine has been in the habit of visiting your classroom after school," the sheriff said. "Is that true?"

"Christine sometimes comes to my classroom to read after school," Standridge said. "She says her father won't let her read at home."

"Would there have been someone else in the classroom who could verify that?" the sheriff said.

"Sometimes there are students in detention," Standridge said.

"We'll need the names of any students who may have observed the two of you together," the sheriff said.

"I'll make a list of those I remember," Standridge told him. "Christine's been coming in most of the year. Less so after the days started getting shorter."

"In the meantime, Lawrence, we're placing you on paid leave until we get this sorted out," the principal said.

"I haven't done anything wrong," Standridge said. A thought occurred to him. "This is retaliation."

"Retaliation for what?" the principal said.

"I've been asking questions about her parents' treatment of her," Standridge said.

"By what authority?" the principal said.

"I've just been asking around on my own," Lawrence said. "I suspected something was wrong and went to the school counselor. He said I'd need more proof than just a feeling."

"That's a matter that should have been handled by the authorities," the principal said.

"Did you learn anything?" the sheriff asked.

"Nothing tangible," Lawrence said. "Messner visited my classroom Friday and made a veiled threat."

"You shouldn't have been poking around in their affairs without authorization," the principal said. "Unfortunately, at this point, it's your word against his."

"Joe, I've been a teacher here for six years," Standridge said. "I have never once been accused of anything like this."

"I'm aware of that, Lawrence," the principal said. "But I'm afraid a formal complaint has been filed, so we can't let you back in the classroom until it's resolved."

"I'm going to need you to come down and answer some questions, as well," the sheriff said.

"Not without an attorney," Standridge said.

"That's your right, sir," the sheriff said. "Still, I will need you to come with me."

At the sheriff's office, Standridge made a phone call to Atlanta and within an hour, an attorney from Macon arrived and advised him not to say anything unless formal charges were brought. The attorney suggested it would be a good idea for Lawrence to take a vacation, maybe head back to Atlanta unless the authorities needed to talk to him, but he chose to remain in town. He was strongly advised to have no contact with the Messners in the meantime.

The Messners restricted access to Christine, not telling the sheriff where she was or when she could be interviewed. At last, the sheriff asked a judge to issue a warrant for her to be brought in as a material witness. Since she was a minor, Zachariah and Selma insisted one or both of them be included in any interview, but the sheriff suspected he'd get more honest responses from Christine if he interviewed her without her parents present. A local attorney came forward to volunteer his services in representing Christine, and after much discussion, the Messners reluctantly agreed to let her speak to the sheriff with the attorney present.

The night before, Zachariah sat Christine down and told her what he expected her to tell the sheriff. He reiterated his instructions as he drove her to the interview, but once she was outside his influence, Christine decided she couldn't lie.

"Christine, I'm going to ask you some questions and I need you to give me an honest response," the sheriff said. "Do you understand?"

"Yes, sir," Christine said. "I wouldn't lie to you about nothing."

"Do you know why you're here?" he said.

"My parents told me I needed to come in here and talk to you," she said. "They been keeping me out of school for the past few days, so I thought it might have something to do with that."

"Your mother has made some accusations against a teacher of yours," the sheriff said.

"A teacher?"

"That's right," he said. "She's said Mr. Standridge has acted inappropriately around you."

"I don't understand," Christine said. "Mr. Standridge hasn't done nothing to me."

"Do you recall spending time with him after school?" the sheriff said.

"I go in his classroom sometime," she said.

"Why is that?"

"To read," she said. "He's got lots of books. My father don't let me read much at home."

"Has he ever had any contact with you while you're there?"

"He talks to me sometimes," she said. "Mostly he just does stuff at his desk while I sit and read."

"Do you like Mr. Standridge, Christine?" the sheriff said.

"Oh yeah," she said. "He's probably about my favorite teacher."

"Why is that?"

"He's always been real nice to me," she said.

"Has he ever put his hands on you?" the sheriff said.

"Put his hands on me?" she said. "I don't understand what you mean. He's shook my hand before. Like in church that one time."

"Have you ever felt uncomfortable around him?"

She lowers her head. "Yeah. Once early on. I used to act up in class to get him to keep me after school, so I could read."

"That's not what I meant," he said. "Does he ever put his hands on you in a way that makes you feel uncomfortable?"

"Mr. Standridge has never put his hands on me at all, except in the way I already said," she tells him. "He's always been a perfect gentleman to me."

"Your mother has told us that she witnessed you in Mr. Standridge's class and that you were upset. Do you recall that?"

"Upset? When did she say this happened?"

"One afternoon when she picked you up at school," the sheriff said.

Christine started laughing. "Picked me up at school? My mama ain't never picked me up at school. I either ride over to Jodie's with her and her mother or I walk home by myself."

"Do your parents treat you okay, Christine?" the sheriff said.

"I guess," she said.

"Do they ever hit you?" he asked.

"Mama sometimes punishes me when I act up," Christine said. "I guess all parents do stuff like that, though."

"Is there anything else you need to know, sheriff?" the attorney said.

"Not at this time," the sheriff said. "Christine, thank you for coming in."

Zachariah and Selma weren't happy that Christine would not confirm what her mother said, but Zachariah insinuated there was another way to teach "that man" to mind his own business without elaborating on what he had in mind. Other students reported nothing out of the ordinary between Standridge and Christine, so Standridge was cleared of the allegations against him. When Christine returned to class, she learned that the local school board was ending Standridge's contract with them, but he would not go into details about why. Christine found him cleaning out his classroom toward the end of the day.

"I'm real sorry about all this Mr. Standridge. I never meant to cause you any trouble."

"None of this is your fault, Christine. I appreciate you telling the truth about me. That was a big help."

"My parents told me to say all sorts of crazy stuff to the sheriff, but I wouldn't do it. You're a good man, Mr. Standridge. You've been a good teacher — and a good friend to me. I'm never going to forget you."

"Obviously, there's not much I can do for you here at this point, but if you ever need anything and I mean anything, look me up in Atlanta and I'll do all I can to help you."

"I will, Mr. Standridge. You take care of yourself.

At the end of that school year, Zachariah pulled Christine out of public school. When Selma balked at trying to teach Christine herself, they enrolled her in a local "Christian Academy" where the students, all women, studied the Bible and learned domestic tasks such as cooking, sewing, and housekeeping. Despite not being in school, Christine still spent afternoons at Jodie's house, following along with her studies.

"Through me you pass into the city of woe: Through me you pass into eternal pain: Through me among the people lost for aye. Justice the founder of my fabric moved: To rear me was the task of Power divine, Supremest Wisdom, and primeval Love. Before me things create were none, save things Eternal, and eternal I endure.
All hope abandon ye who enter here."
--Dante, *The Divine Comedy: Inferno*

Second Christine

The Fall of James Frederick

Between age fourteen and fifteen, Christine underwent a transformation and suddenly grew more than a foot and lost most of the weight she'd carried as a child. Now she was taller than both her parents, slender, and she let her hair grow out, and most who'd known her all her life found it difficult to believe the chubby and awkward duckling had grown into such a beautiful swan. One person who noticed was James Frederick and Christine noted a change in his attitude toward her. He had always been friendly and had taken an interest in what she had to tell him. Now he became more overtly affectionate, greeting her with extended hugs or touching her shoulder when they talked, or putting his arm around her if she was standing near him.

His actions toward her had not escaped the notice of Zachariah, who took a particular interest in the many times Frederick would blush, or stammer whenever Christine was around. In these instances, he would often show uncharacteristic camaraderie with Frederick, cracking a joke about the heat, or inquiring about Paul's writings on lust in the heart. Messner's attitude toward Christine seemed to soften as well and he started asking her questions about boys she might like or how she spent her time when away from the house. Peppered in with these inquiries were mentions of Frederick and how he behaved around her.

Christine and Jodie always had an affectionate relationship. There wasn't anything erotic about it, and if either of them was aware of the concept of women in love affairs with one another, which their sheltered upbringing dictated against, they most likely would have regarded it as weird, silly, or ungodly. If either had been asked, they'd have stated their goals were to one day marry and start families, just as many in their community expected them to do. The only person likely to misunderstand or take issue with it was Zachariah Messner. As long as they were young girls, their affection toward one another went unnoticed, but once they became attractive young women, Messner took note of it more and more, and Jodie's name came up frequently in his questions about Christine's activities.

One afternoon, just after Christine turned sixteen years old, she arrived home to find Zachariah and Selma waiting for her in the living room. The looks on their faces told her something was wrong, and she wracked her brain to try to remember what she might have done to set them off.

"What's going on?" she asked, only to have Zachariah bark at her to sit down.

She sat in a chair that had been pulled in from the dining room.

"What's going on with you and that Newcombe girl, and don't lie to me," Zachariah said, hovering just a few inches from Christine's face.

"Nothing's going on," Christine said. "We're friends."

"Friends," Zachariah hissed. "That's what they're calling it now, is it?"

"I don't know what you're talking about," Christine said, her fear growing. "We ain't done nothing."

"I said don't lie to me, girl," Zachariah said. "We saw you two, holding hands, hugging on one another. You call that nothing?"

"It don't mean nothing," Christine said. "All girls do that."

"Liar," Selma said. "I never done nothing like that when I was your age."

Zachariah produced a Bible and held it out. "You put your hand on this Bible, girl, and you swear to me you ain't one of those lesbians."

"A what?" Christine said. "I don't even know what that is."

"You swear, girl!" he said. "Or things are going to get a lot worse for you."

"I can't swear to not be something if I don't know what it is," she said.

"That's enough for me," Zachariah said to Selma.

They grabbed Christine by either arm and hustled her into the back of the house to the large storage closet. They pushed her inside, slammed the door, and she could hear them closing the latch and locking it. She sat there in almost total darkness for a very long time. The only illumination was from under the door and that was just the light fixtures in the kitchen which hardly provided enough light to do anything. She tried to feel around in the dark but came to realize her parents had cleared out the room before putting her there, because all she felt were empty shelves.

Jodie rushed to get dressed, anxious to get to church that day. She was hoping to see Christine, who she had not seen or heard from since Jodie walked her home nearly a week ago. Not only had Christine not been to Jodie's house, but she had not called either, which was totally out of character for her. Jodie worried more when she arrived at church to find Selma and Zachariah seated in their usual pew without Christine.

"Daddy, I'm worried about Christine," she whispered to her father. "I haven't heard from her for days and now she's not at church. That's not like her."

"I'll ask Deacon Messner about her after the service, honey," Mr. Newcombe said.

Once the service concluded, Jodie and her father approached Zachariah and Selma as they were leaving.

"Afternoon Deacon," Newcombe said. "Selma. Is everything okay with Christine? We noticed she's not in church."

"What concern is it of yours?" Zachariah said.

"Christine's my friend," Jodie said. "I haven't heard from her in days. I'm worried."

"There's nothing for you to worry about, girl," Zachariah said. "She's just gone out of town is all. Visiting relatives in Moultrie."

"But she usually calls me," Jodie said.

"Maybe they ain't got any phones down there, you stop to think about that?" Selma said.

"Jodie's worried about her friend," Newcombe said. "I'm a bit worried about her too, if we're being honest."

"I said there's nothing to worry about," Messner said. "I'll see if I can get in touch with the home folks down there. Have her call you."

"That would be good," Newcombe said. "That suit you, Jodie?"

"Yes, sir," Jodie said. "That'd be a relief."

Later that evening, Jodie answered the phone to be greeted by Christine's voice.

"Hey Jodie. Heard you was asking about me."

While Jodie was sure it was Christine, something in how she spoke sounded different, strained, like she was scared.

"Christine, are you all right?" Jodie said. "You just disappeared."

"It's okay. I'm down in Waycross visiting folks. Nothing to worry about."

"Your father said you were in Moultrie," Jodie said.

"He must have just got mixed up," Christine said. "We got family both places."

"When are you coming home?"

"Don't know yet," Christine said. "Maybe not for a while."

A thought comes to Jodie. "Is somebody there with you, Christine?"

"Of course. I told you I'm visiting relatives. They're all over the place."

"Are you safe where you are, Christine?"

"Why wouldn't I be? I'm with my family."

"You're not really in Waycross or Moultrie, are you?" Jodie said.

"I got to go now, Jodie," Christine said. "Don't know when I can talk to you again. They ain't got no phones down here. I hope I see you again."

The line disconnects.

"Christine?"

Jodie went to her parents and told them about the call. The next day, her father went by the sheriff's office, who told him that since her parents had not reported her missing, and had an explanation for where she was, there wasn't much he could do, but the sheriff agreed to drive by the Messners' house and ask some questions. When he did, he talked to Selma, and didn't find anything out of the ordinary.

Christine was in complete darkness as she had been for longer than she could recall. Her parents had yet to tell her specifically what she had done to earn their wrath but had none-the-less carried it out without hesitation or cessation. She was still wearing the dress she had on when they placed her in the storage closet, though they took away her shoes after she tried to kick open the door, and her hands were often bound behind her after she tried banging on the wall to attract attention. She had been beaten on her back and thighs, with belts, sticks, wire clothes hangers, and anything else her parents could find to cause her pain, and as a result, she had to lie on her side to rest. Twice a day, her mother would lead her, blindfolded, to the bathroom, so she could take care of any necessities, and her mother waited there with her until she was finished. Once a day, she'd be supplied with a tiny amount of food and water, which she had to consume in darkness. As a result, her weight had declined significantly.

With each beating, usually carried out by her mother, her father would stand by reciting verses from the Bible, but with no specific pattern that allowed Christine to ascertain what she was expected to learn from the ordeal. For most of her time, she was left alone, unable to see or speak to anyone. She filled these times with prayer for her deliverance. She found reciting Psalm 23 to be of particular comfort for her.

This night, something was different. Her mother unlocked the door and took Christine to her room where she was ordered to put on a dress Selma had chosen for her. Told not to say or try anything, she was then led into the living room, where her suitcase was sitting by the couch. Selma shoved Christine onto the couch with instructions not to speak or move. A short while later, Zachariah returned home, and, seeing Christine, said, "She ready?"

"She is," Selma said.

"Take her things to the car," Zachariah instructed Selma.

As Selma complied, Zachariah crouched down so he was face to face with Christine.

"You listen to me and listen good, girl," he said. "We're going to get in the car and drive. You don't look at nobody. You don't talk to nobody. You do anything out of the ordinary, and you're never going to be seen alive again, you understand?"

Christine nodded.

"Good," Messner said. "Let's go."

He pulled her off the couch and led her out to the car. Selma was waiting beside the open passenger door and remained there after Zachariah pushed Christine in, slammed the door, and got behind the wheel, then she went back into the house. Zachariah drove into town to a house Christine recognized.

"Deacon Frederick," she said to herself as Zachariah pulled into the driveway. Her spirits lifted a bit. Messner made her carry her suitcase up the walk as he remained behind her. She rang the bell.

When he came to the door, Frederick stared at Christine in disbelief.

"Christine. Thank the good Lord. Are you all right?"

"Good as can be," Christine said as she entered.

Frederick turned to Messner. "What did you do to her?"

"What needed to be done," Messner said. "No matter. She's your problem now."

Christine looked between them. "What does he mean?"

"You're going to live here, Christine," Frederick said. "Help out with the chores. Do some cooking."

"Really?" Christine said, the excitement evident in her voice.

"For now," Frederick said. "We may look at making it permanent if things work out."

"I'll be on my way then," Messner said, heading toward the door.

"Don't come back," Frederick said.

For the first few days after coming to Deacon Frederick's house, Christine moved about tentatively, always asking permission to leave her room. Frederick suggested it would be best if she not go outside or talk to any of the neighbors to protect her from any untoward rumors, and Christine agreed. He also suggested she not attend church services, so as not to encounter her parents, and she gratefully agreed to that as well. Instead, they had a weekly devotional in place of service. She busied herself by cleaning up around the house and preparing meals. She worried that if she did not do as she was told, Frederick would send her back to the Messners. At last, Frederick allayed her fears.

"Even if things don't work out here, I'm not sending you back to them, Christine," Frederick told her. "We'll just work out some other arrangement."

"An arrangement for what Deacon Frederick?" Christine said.

"You don't need to worry about that right now, Christine," Frederick said. "Just know you're safe under my roof, okay?"

These were the words Christine had always wanted to hear from him. For the first time in her life, she felt protected and secure and began to open up to Frederick. She'd dutifully remain in his house during the day tidying up, start dinner cooking about a half an hour before he was scheduled to arrive home, and sit at the table with him discussing the day's events once he was back. She even began showing some innocent affection for him, giving him occasional hugs, such as when he arrived home in the afternoon, or spontaneously while they were sitting on the couch together. Sometimes she'd reward him with a simple peck on the cheek. In her mind, it's how a teenaged daughter should respond to her father, and that's how she had come to regard Deacon Frederick: as the father she'd never before had.

Christine came to realize Frederick did not think of her in the same manner.

He began to reciprocate Christine's shows of affection, bringing her flowers or little trinkets in the afternoon, which she gratefully accepted, and he, too, had begun to spontaneously hug her and steal quick kisses whenever she was close. At times she felt uncomfortable with an extended hug, or when a kiss landed a little too close to her lips. She was especially uncomfortable with the times he'd drop into her room with little more than a knock and catch her not fully clothed.

One evening, while Christine was reading in bed — Frederick had been very generous in supplying her with the books she requested that her father would have forbidden — Frederick looked in on her. Something in his manner was different. He seemed nervous and jumpy. Christine had observed a similar attitude among some of the boys she'd noticed when she was attending school whenever they were around girls they were dating, but the manner didn't seem to fit Deacon Frederick. He indicated her bed and said, "Can I join you?"

"Okay," she said, sitting up and letting her legs drape over the side of the bed. She set her book on the bedside table. He sat beside her, closer than he usually did. Christine chuckled a bit and said, "What's going on."

"Christine, I just wanted to say how special it's been having you here in this house the past few weeks," Frederick said. "When your father brought you here, I had doubts about the arrangement he proposed, but I can see now he was right."

"Right about what?" Christine said.

"About us," he said. "You know I've always loved you."

"I love you too, Deacon Frederick," Christine said.

"Don't you think you should call me James, Christine?" he said.

"If you want me to. I guess I could."

"I never believed we'd have a life together," he said. "Now I see we can. Thank you for showing me that."

"Thank you for letting me live in your house," she said.

"Our house, Christine," Frederick said. "It's our house now."

"Pleased to hear that, Deacon — I mean — James. I'm happy you let me come here and work for you."

"I hope you don't feel that's the only reason you're here, Christine," he said.

"I don't understand," Christine said. "Why else would I be here?"

He put his arm around her. Something didn't feel right to her.

"To be my wife," Frederick said.

Before she could fully process this, Frederick leaned against her and pressed his lips to hers. This caused her to fall back onto the bed. He climbed beside her and pulled her up onto the bed with him.

"What are you doing?" she said, the fright evident in her voice.

"It's okay," he said. "I know it's not official yet, but that doesn't' matter. We're the only ones who need to know about it."

He placed his hand on her stomach and slowly moved it down to between her legs.

"Stop it," she said, hysterically. "Don't do this."

"You don't need to be frightened," Frederick said. "I understand what you've been telling me. There's nothing to be ashamed of, Christine. I love you."

He kissed her again, and as he did, he pulled her panties down and began to loosen his belt.

"Deacon Frederick don't do this," she cried out. "James! I don't want this."

He moved so his body was partially covering hers. She tried but couldn't get out from under him.

"It's natural to be a little hesitant your first time," Frederick said. "But soon it's all going to be okay."

He pulled her closer and positioned himself over her, while she continued to struggle. When he penetrated her, she let out a sustained scream, which devolved into heavy sobs.

It's how he left her once he was done.

Christine sat on the bed, her arms wrapped around herself, head down, with her eyes focused on the door. Since Frederick left, a single thought had gone through her mind.

I didn't do anything.

It was both an admonishment to herself for not trying harder to get away — though she knew she had tried as hard as she could — and an answer to the question she kept coming back to, "What did I do?" She had mentally run through everything she could recall saying and all her actions from the time she first came to live here, examining each interaction they'd had, wondering what might have sparked Frederick's actions. She gritted her teeth then said aloud, "I didn't do anything."

There was a knock at the door, followed by Frederick calling her name. She remained silent, staring at the door. He knocked again, then opened the door and stepped into the room. Seeing him, she crawled to the far side of the bed, and positioned herself against the wall, pulling her legs to her chest and wrapping her arms around them. He stopped, just inside the door, and held up his hand.

"I'm not going to touch you again, Christine," he told her. "I see now you weren't ready, and it was wrong of me to force myself on you. I apologize."

"What'd you think was going to happen?"

"Honestly, I didn't know," he said. "Perhaps I misread your signals."

"I wasn't sending you no signals," she said.

"Maybe you just didn't realize it," he said. "You've been very affectionate. Very open. How was I supposed to read that?"

"I was being nice. I was happy you let me stay here. I wasn't sending no signals. Especially for you to do what you did."

"I've said I'm sorry and I am."

"Just let me go," she said. "Please."

"I can't let you go, Christine. You're my responsibility now, and I take that very seriously."

"Deacon Frederick, please—"

"You should call me James, Christine."

"Please! Just let me go."

"Get some rest," Frederick continued. "We can talk about this tomorrow."

Christine couldn't sleep. She just laid awake, constantly watching the door, listening for footsteps in the hall that would warn her if he was coming back. Before sunrise, she crept out of bed and hurriedly dressed, then got back into bed and pulled the covers over her.

When Frederick looked in, she told him she wasn't feeling well and stayed in bed until she heard his car pull away. She leapt out from under the covers, rushed out the back door and went to the only place she knew to go, her parent's house, where she knew she'd find her mother, alone.

Selma was in the kitchen when Christine got to the house, and let herself in. Hearing the door, Selma came in and wasn't happy to see Christine.

"What you doing here?" she said. "Does Deacon Frederick know you're gone?"

"No, Mama, I ran away."

"What you do that for?" Selma said. "You're supposed to stay there. You're lucky Zachariah ain't here. He'd have a fit."

"Mama, you can't send me back to him. He did things to me. He put his — his — in me."

"Well, of course he did," Selma said. "He's going to be your husband. Didn't they explain that to you?"

"Husband? You know about that?"

"Course I do. It ain't official yet, but that's the deal. You didn't think he was just doing this out of the kindness of his heart, did you?"

"I got to go," Christine said, starting toward the door. "I made a mistake coming here."

Selma blocked her. "No, you don't." She pushed Christine into the back and shoved her into the storage closet, locking it. Then she called Frederick.

Once he got her back to his house, Frederick said, "Christine, you can't run off like that again. I know this is an unusual situation, but it's for the best all around."

"Is what you did last night for the best?" Christine said.

"I have already apologized for that," he said. "I now understand you weren't ready and didn't see things the way I did."

"But you're going to do it again, aren't you?" she said.

"Not until you're ready," he told her.

"What if I'm never ready?"

"It's what a husband and wife do, Christine. It's what I'm going to expect of you once we're married. Not right now, but eventually. Do you understand?"

She just stared at him with a mixture of horror and anger.

The following day, Christine ran away again. She went to the bus station and tried to buy a ticket to where her uncle Alvin lived. A woman from her church, who worked there, saw her and called Selma, who called Frederick. In retaliation, Frederick locked up all her clothes, so all she had was the dress she was wearing.

The third time, Christine went to the sheriff's office and they called Zachariah. When he arrived, Christine begged the police not to turn her over to him.

"Don, the girl's been a problem as long as she's been under my roof," Messner said. "I thought sending her away to our relatives would help but it only made the problem worse when she got back. She's started rebelling against my authority."

"She looks to me like she's scared to death, Zachariah," the sheriff said.

"I am," Christine said.

"Hush up, girl," Zachariah snapped at her. "It's all her, Don. We put food in front of her and she won't eat it. We try to get her to go to church and she throws a fit. The girl recoils from the very word of the Lord when I try to read her passages from the Bible.

I've never encountered anyone so willful, or contemptuous of the Lord."

"That's not true," Christine said.

"See what I mean?" Zachariah said. "One lie after another."

"And you're sure she's not suffering any psychological issues?" the sheriff asked. "We could send her over to the medical center for an evaluation if you'd like."

"Yes. Send me there," Christine said. "Just don't give me back to him."

"Trust me when I say, there's nothing wrong with her mind. It's her soul that's gone astray," Zachariah said. "You know me, Don. I've always run a strict household. It's what the Lord commands. This is just a test to my authority, and I cannot let her win."

"All right," the sheriff said. "We'll go ahead and let you take her. But if she shows up here again, I'll have to call DFACS."

"She won't be a problem anymore," Messner said.

Christine was near hysterics. "No! Don't give me back to him."

"Quiet down," Messner said. "Show some respect for yourself even if you refuse to respect me."

He led her out to his car and drove her back to Frederick's. Frederick was waiting for him beside his house.

"Bring her back here," Frederick said. He led them to a small tool shed. "Put her here for now."

"No!" Christine said as Messner pushed her into the shed. Frederick closed and bolted the door after her. She tried calling out, but the walls were reinforced.

Several hours later, when Frederick led Christine back into the house, she found he had put in a steel plate, brackets, and braces. Before she had time to fully process what its purpose was, he put a brace on her right ankle attached to a chain which he locked to the bracket on the wall.

"You're locking me up like a dog?" Christine said.

"You're very willful, Christine," he said, "very headstrong. I need to insure you don't try to run away again. You can't afford any more run-ins with your father."

"Just let me go," she pleaded. "I ain't your wife and I ain't going to be your wife, no matter how long you keep me chained up. I promise I won't tell nobody what you did if you just let me go."

"Over time, you're going to learn just how much I care for you, Christine. When that time comes, I will welcome you as my devoted wife. But until then, I need to insure you're going to remain in my care. One day you'll thank me."

Christine started pounding on the wall and screaming.

"Christine, stop that," Frederick said. "Stop it now."

Christine ignored him and screamed louder. Frederick moved toward her.

"Christine, I said stop!"

Christine turned to face him.

"Or what?"

Frederick unhooked his belt, removed, and folded it.

Christine started to scream again, pounding and kicking the wall. Frederick went to her, forced her against the wall and began whipping her with his belt.

In the weeks after she was chained up, Frederick began visiting Christine in the evening to read the Bible to her. She noted that he always selected passages that emphasized a woman's responsibility to her husband. While he generally promoted the teachings of Paul, Frederick would often hesitate when he encountered passages dealing with Paul's stated preference for celibacy, often skipping to another passage.

Since being beaten with his belt, Christine acted much more complacent, sitting on the ground, staring at the floor, while Frederick read the Scripture. She hadn't been eating, except for a few morsels each day, when she was really hungry; she had not bathed in more than a week, and she rarely spoke to him. Underneath her silent facade, however, her mind was working overtime, the single, guiding thought being, *I didn't do anything. I don't deserve this.*

She considered her life, all the times she had silently endured the verbal and physical abuse inflicted on her by her parents, the taunts of her classmates at how she dressed, the unspoken disapproval shown on the faces of many of those who attended her church. She thought about the number of times she had wished she could live with Deacon Frederick and be a family. Now he was treating her like his property that he could lock up and treat however he wished. She could not understand what had changed from the friendly man she'd known when she was younger, but something had changed and her admiration of him now turned to pure hatred and disgust. She began to formulate a plan.

I don't deserve this.

Finally, one evening during his Bible reading, she broke her silence.

"James, do you think, maybe you could let me out of these chains?"

"Why would I do that, Christine?"

"I was just thinking how much I'd like to fix dinner for my husband."

"I'd like to believe that, Christine," he said, leaning toward her.

"You can believe it — James," she replied. "I been sitting her thinking what the Lord would want, and I can't explain his mysteries — but he brought me to you for a reason. I see that now. I understand that you know what's best for me and I want to apologize for being such a problem."

"It's okay, Christine. I forgive you."

"So, I just thought maybe we could start over and I could cook something for you. It'd be my honor to do that."

Frederick set the Bible on a table, rose, and took out his key chain.

"You don't know how happy I am to hear you say that, Christine. I haven't wanted to be this tough. You know that, right?"

"I understand. You was only doing it for my own good. I was willful and thinking only of myself, but I'd like to try again, if that's okay with you."

Frederick unchained her and helped her to her feet, then embraced her.

"That would be wonderful, Christine."

Frederick followed Christine to the door of the kitchen. She stopped outside and put up her hand.

"No, you just sit down and relax. I know my way around okay. It's a wife's duty to serve her husband."

"The back door's barred, Christine," Frederick told her. "You can't get out that way."

"I guess I deserve that. Let me show you I'm worthy of your trust."

"Very well, Christine."

Christine watched as Frederick sat at the dining room table with his back to the door then entered the kitchen. She rattled some pots and pans and turned on the water in the faucet. She opened the drawer that held the knives, took out the butcher knife, and held it up, then looked again toward the door. Her eyes fell on the heavy, cast iron frying pan on the stove and she put away the knife and closed the drawer.

"I'm really looking forward to this, Christine," Frederick called to her. "What's on the menu?"

She gripped the frying pan with both hands.

"I ain't going to say just now. I need to see what you've got to work with. Plus, I want it to be a surprise."

She exited into the dining room and crept up behind Frederick until she was very close.

"I'm sure it's going to be delicious," he called out. "I can't wait."

"You ain't got to wait no more," Christine said as she swung the pan toward his head. The pan connected with the right side of his face which caused him to fall sideways off his chair, with a loud grunt. He put his hand to his head and focused on her bare feet as she raised the pan high above her. He looked up and before he could say or do anything, she screamed, and brought the frying pan down on his head. He crumpled beneath her.

Christine dropped the pan and moved to Frederick's side, fishing in his pockets for his keys. She found them and went into the kitchen and opened the padlock that secured the bar across the door, removed it and tossed it aside.

"I hope you ain't dead," she said, looking at Frederick then tossed the keys toward him. She flung open the back door and fled into the darkness. There was only one place she could think to go.

Christine lurked in the shadows beside the Newcombe residence, until she saw Jodie walking toward the house. She called out Jodie's name and when Jodie stopped, she emerged from the shadows and moved slowly toward her. Frightened, Jodie backed away toward her front door, but as Christine moved into the light, Jodie recognized her.

"Christine?" she said. "My sweet Lord, what have they done to you?"

"Almost killed me," Christine said as she fell into Jodie's arms. They embraced, both breaking into tears.

"You got to hide me," Christine said. "I ran away from Deacon Frederick. Hit him in the head with a pan. He may be dead for all I know."

"Come on, I'll take you in the back, so the neighbors won't see us," Jodie said. "My parents are at the church tonight. I'm supposed to join them once I get changed, but I'll help you all I can beforehand."

They went around back and into the house. Jodie took Christine to her room.

"What were you doing at Deacon Frederick's?" Jodie asked.

"My father took me there," Christine said. "Deacon Frederick told me I was going to be his wife."

"What? That doesn't make any sense. What happened?"

"He forced himself on me, Jodie," Christine told her. "Said he was sorry afterward, but said he was going to do it again."

"That doesn't sound like Deacon Frederick."

"I didn't think so either, but I swear to you it happened. Told me that's what a man and wife do."

"Christine, we've got to get you to a hospital."

"No! You take me there they'll call my parents. If they get their hands on me, they'll either take me back to Deacon Frederick or worse."

"What would be worse than that?"

"You won't never see me again. Understand?"

"You think they'd kill you?"

"Look at me! What do you think?"

Jodie nods.

"You should at least get out of these clothes. Take a bath."

Christine removed the dress. Underneath, she was only wearing panties. On her shoulders, back, and thighs were bruises, welts, and scars. Jodie gasped when she saw them.

"My Lord, Christine. Did Deacon Frederick do that to you too?"

"Some of it," Christine said. "My parents did most of it before they took me there."

"I'm going to get the camera," Jodie said. "Take some pictures."

"No. I don't want nobody to see it."

"You got to, Christine," Jodie told her. "You need proof. Otherwise they'll deny it happened."

Christine consented. Jodie got her family's Polaroid and used up two photo packets taking pictures of the scars and bruises. Then she took Christine to the bathroom with some towels and waited outside while Christine bathed.

"I don't think I got any clothes will fit you," Jodie told Christine once they were back in Jodie's room. "Maybe Buddy has some jeans you can wear."

"Won't he miss 'em?" Christine said.

"I'll get some old ones out of his bottom drawer," Jodie says. "He only wears those when he runs out of new ones. I'll get you one of his T-shirts, too."

Buddy Newcombe was several inches taller than Christine, so his jeans fit her legs, though they were very loose around the waist and Christine had to use one of Jodie's belts and cinch it tightly to keep them from falling off her. His T-shirt totally engulfed her slender frame, but she was thankful to, at last, have some clean clothes on.

Jodie brought her an assortment of luncheon meats, cheeses, and bread, then said, "I need to get on to the church. Just stay in my room, and if anybody comes home that you don't want to talk to, hide in the closet."

"I will."

"When I get a chance, I'll say something to my father," Jodie said. "He'll know what to do."

Once the family returned home that night, Jody brought Christine out to tell them what she'd gone through. Seeing her, Mr. and Mrs. Newcombe were as shocked as Jodie had been at her condition, more so when Jodie showed them the photos she took.

As they were discussing what would happen next, there was a knock at the door and Mrs. Newcombe looked to see it was the sheriff. Christine and Jodie went into Jodie's room while Mr. and Mrs. Newcombe spoke to him. Christine could hear the sheriff explaining that the Messners suggested she might have come here when he went by to investigate a robbery and assault at James Frederick's house. They called the girls out and all sat at the dining room table while Christine repeated her story to the sheriff.

"James Frederick is in the hospital right now," the sheriff said. "He managed to call an ambulance after he woke up from the assault, and the hospital called us. His skull is cracked, and he's heavily sedated, so, consequently, he hasn't been very helpful in sorting out what happened. All he could tell the deputies is that you attacked him in his home. I spoke to your parents and they said they sent you there to work."

"That's what they told me, sir," Christine said. "Deacon Frederick said we was supposed to get married and my Mama confirmed that."

"We did find some sort of chain apparatus in one of the bedrooms as you mentioned, so we're going to have quite a few questions for him whenever he's more coherent. In the meantime, we'll need to take you into custody until we sort all this out."

"You ain't going to give me back to my parents, are you?" she said.

"Given what you've told us, it sounds like the county's going to need to get involved," the sheriff said. "You'll probably need to go into juvenile detention or foster care until we sort everything out."

Mr. Newcombe addressed the sheriff.

"Don, there's no reason at all to take her out of here tonight. She's safe under our roof. Let her get a good night's sleep. We'll bring her by first thing in the morning."

"All right, Bobby. I don't see any harm in that."

Mr. Newcombe went to Christine and cupped her hand in both of his. He pressed something into her palm.

"Christine, we love you and want to help you all we can," he said, "but this situation is beyond our capabilities. Tomorrow morning, I'm taking you over to the sheriff, who's better equipped to handle all this."

Christine lowered her head. "Yes sir, Mr. Newcombe."

"It's for the best," Newcombe said.

"That'll be fine," the sheriff said. "Y'all have a nice evening."

"We'll walk out with you Don, so we can work out the details," Newcombe said.

Mr. and Mrs. Newcombe and the sheriff left. Jodie went to Christine and touched her shoulder.

"Christine, I'm so sorry. I thought for sure my father would help you."

Christine smiled and brought up her hand, holding several folded twenty-dollar bills.

"Your father did help."

"What are you going to do?" Jodie asks.

"I got to get to Atlanta," Christine said. "Mr. Standridge said if I needed anything to come find him there."

Jodie shook her head. "I can't get you to Atlanta, but I can take you to Macon tonight after everybody's asleep."

"That's enough. I should be able to get a bus from there. Ain't nobody in Macon will recognize me."

That night, after the family went to bed, Christine put some clothes in an overnight bag and she and Jodie took the family car into Macon. Jodie dropped her off at the Greyhound station and gave her a long hug.

"You take care of yourself, Christine," she said. She took Christine's hands and they bowed their heads, "Dear Lord, watch over Christine and guide her journey."

"Amen," Christine said. She and Jodie embraced once more. "I'll find a way to let you know where I am when I get to Atlanta. Tell your father I said thanks. When you can."

"I will."

With that, they parted. Christine purchased a ticket for an express bus that left at four forty-five in the morning. By the time

Mr. Newcombe was at the sheriff's, explaining how Christine somehow slipped away in the night, she was disembarking at the Greyhound station in downtown Atlanta.

She had no idea how to contact Mr. Standridge. She knew his name was Lawrence, but there weren't any listed in the Atlanta phone book, though there were several with the initial "L". Finally, she took out some change and started dialing. After many tries, she finally reached a sleepy sounding teenager who said his uncle was named Lawrence and he used to be a teacher down around Macon.

"Could you tell me how to get in touch with him?" she said. "It's real important."

"I have his number, but there's nobody there now," he said. "He's out of town until Sunday."

He offered to give her the number for his grandfather, which she gladly accepted. She rang up the elder Mr. Standridge, and once she explained herself to him and said why she was looking for his son, he agreed to come to the station with his wife to pick her up. Hardly an hour later, an older couple arrived, the man with silver hair and a bushy mustache, wearing a U.S. Marine Corps baseball cap, and the woman with dark hair streaked with grey, who was the very image of the Mr. Standridge Christine remembered. They took her back to their house in Avondale, got her some breakfast, and set her up in a guest room.

"I'm going to call Larry this afternoon to let him know you're here," Mrs. Standridge told her. "They're a few hours behind us on the West Coast."

A few nights later, Lawrence and Christine were reunited at his parents' home. When he walked in, he hardly recognized the tall, thin woman who greeted him with enthusiasm. Christine now towered over him.

After dinner, they sat on his parents' back porch while she told him all that had happened to her and why she had sought him out.

"Look, my — ah — friend — my roommate, that is — he's a civil rights attorney. He'll know how to help you get out of this mess."

"I'd be grateful for his assistance," Christine said.

"My parents say it's okay for you to stay here for the time being," Standridge said. "That might be the best, since the authorities may realize you headed this way. Mom wants to take you out and get you some new clothes."

"I'll welcome their hospitality," she said. "I like your parents."

Over the next several days, Christine met with Lawrence and his friend, Elijah Parker, and described the treatment she received at the hands of her parents and Deacon Frederick. As she spent more time with the pair, she began to realize they weren't just friends.

"It's true, isn't it?" she asked Lawrence. "What people was saying about you after you left Perry. You're a sodomite."

"That's not what we prefer to be called," Elijah said.

"Let me handle it, Eli," Lawrence said. "Christine, it's true. I'm gay. It's who I am."

"But the Bible says—" Christine began.

"Oh, here we go with the Bible."

"Not now, Eli," Lawrence said. "You know me, Christine. Have I ever done anything to make you doubt how much I care about you?"

"No sir, you haven't," Christine said, still unable to look at him.

"Then that's all you need to know about me," he replied. "We're here to help you, and we'll do everything we can to protect you."

She looked up and met his eyes. "You're right. I know I can trust you. It might take me a while to get past the other thing, but I know you're my friend. That's what matters."

"What about me?" Elijah said.

Christine shrugs. "Mr. Standridge says you're okay. I guess I can believe him."

"I can live with that," Elijah said with a chuckle.

"You know me well enough to at least call me Lawrence, Christine," he said. "Mr. Standridge is my father."

"He told me to call him Jack," she said.

"Okay, my grandfather, then," Standridge said.

They laughed.

Elijah enlisted the aid of some people in his office to ascertain the situation Christine left behind in Perry. At their next meeting, he outlined what he discovered.

"An associate at my office contacted a colleague in Macon who drove down and talked to the sheriff," Elijah told her. "You have assault charges pending against you by James Frederick. The story he's given the sheriff's office is that he hired you to work in his house and you robbed him and assaulted him."

"That's a lie and he knows it," Christine said.

"Fortunately, evidence inside his house contradicted his account and your friend Jodie came forward with photos showing your injuries and he's not offered a convincing explanation for that," Elijah went on. "Still, he's claiming it was your parents who caused most of your injuries, not him. He says that's what prompted him to take you in."

"That's mostly true, I guess. What does that mean for me?"

"The fact that you're sixteen weighs in your favor," Elijah said. "If you're convicted in juvenile court, it means they can only hold you until you're eighteen."

"I don't want to go to jail," she said. "Not even for two years. I didn't do anything wrong. What about my parents."

"They've put out a bulletin looking for you," Elijah said. He opens his briefcase and removes a flyer. "Here's the flyer that's being sent out to the state."

The flyer contained a general description of Christine, and a photo from when she was thirteen.

"That doesn't look anything like you now," Lawrence said.

"It's the last school picture I had taken," Christine said.

"Since you're a minor, you'll need someone to represent you," Elijah said. "You can go to court and ask that Lawrence, or someone else, be appointed your guardian. Jack and Nancy Standridge have indicated they'd be happy to do so. The other option is that you could petition the court for emancipation."

"Emancipation? Like when they freed the slaves?" Christine said.

"Similar concept," Elijah said. "You'd be able to make your own decisions without an adult."

"That sounds good to me," Christine said. "What I need to do?"

"You have to apply in juvenile court in your county of residence," Elijah told her.

"Houston County? Won't they arrest me?"

"It's a definite possibility," Elijah said. "The sheriff thinks a judge would be lenient in sentencing, if it goes that far, given the special circumstances."

"I'll go. There's nothing they can do to me that's any worse than what they already done."

"Are you sure about this, Christine?" Lawrence said.

"If it means being free of those people, I'll walk through hell itself."

"We'll be there with you, Christine," Lawrence said. "You don't have to worry."

She took both their hands.

"I'm sorry how I reacted when I found out about the two of you. Everybody always told me all sorts of bad things about homosexuals when I was growing up, I didn't know what to think. Truth is, you two are about the only men in my life who ever stood up for me. I'll always be grateful for that."

"Thank you, Christine," Elijah said. "We're with you all the way."

Christine, Lawrence, and Elijah arrived in Perry to learn that the charges against her had been dropped. Later, at a reunion at Jodie's home, her father revealed he had a talk with Deacon Frederick and convinced him there was no need in punishing Christine further.

"I let him know there were some photos in evidence that showed some of her injuries were more recent to the time she ran away," Newcombe said. "After some reflection, he said the Lord touched his heart and he reconsidered."

"Thank you, Mr. Newcombe," Christine said.

"I just wish we knew more about what was going on in time to spare you all that," Jodie said.

"You helped me a lot," Christine said, hugging her friend. "Without you and your family, I might not be alive now."

"Your parents have stated they want you returned to them," Elijah said. "I filed an injunction blocking them from proceeding until we have our day in court. I'd recommend we take care of that as quickly as we can."

Within a few days, Christine's motion was filed, and each party was called on to give evidence in the case. When Christine met Lawrence and Elijah for their afternoon briefing later that week, Elijah seemed subdued. He explained he'd been in depositions since last evening, including Selma Messner.

"There's something you need to know, Christine," Elijah said. "In your mother's deposition yesterday evening, she admitted to an indiscretion, as she called it."

"An indiscretion?" Christine asked.

"Some years ago, around the time you were conceived," Elijah went on. "She's pretty sure Zachariah Messner isn't your father."

A horrifying thought crossed Christine's mind. "Not my father. Who is? Did she say?"

Elijah wouldn't face her. "James Frederick."

"Deacon Frederick? My father? All those things he did to me?"

"Your mother said he never knew," Elijah said. "She never told him. Lied about when you were conceived."

Christine looked away, considering all she'd been told. "Is there any chance I can see him? Talk to him?"

"Why would you want to?" Lawrence said.

"I got my reasons. I want to let him know I forgive him. It's what the Lord would want me to do."

"After all you've been through, you still believe God had a hand in this, Christine?" Lawrence said.

"Course I do," she said. "It's my faith that's got me through all this. That's why I want to talk to Deacon Frederick. To let him know that while I don't understand what led him down the path he took, it's not for me to judge him."

Elijah looked down and cleared his throat. "Frederick didn't show up for his deposition this morning. When the deputies went to pick him up, they found him in his garage. He hung himself."

Tears streamed down Christine's cheeks. "I used to wish he was my daddy. That I could go live in his house and be his little girl. Now I wish I didn't even have to have a father. That I could have just been born out of thin air, like in them fairy tales."

Elijah went on, "The neighbors said the last time they saw Frederick, he was on the front porch yesterday evening having a heated discussion with Messner."

"Couldn't wait," Christine said. "He just had to run and tell him. I guess in the end, he won, didn't he?"

"He hasn't defeated you, Christine," Lawrence said.

"He's not going to neither," she replied. "The only good to come from all this is knowing that monster ain't my kin."

By the end of the week, the evidence gathering for the trial was over and all the parties assembled in juvenile court for a ruling. The only people not in attendance were Zachariah and Selma Messner.

"Mr. Solomon, we are waiting," the judge said to the Messners' attorney. "When can we expect your clients."

"Your honor, my clients have informed me they won't be attending court today."

"They are aware that they are legally required to be here," the judge said, "are they not?"

"I stressed that to them, your honor."

"Then why aren't they here?" the judge said.

"Your honor, they left word at my office that I am to say they are in mourning for the death of their daughter."

An audible gasp went through the courtroom. Christine looked away and covered her face. Elijah put his arm around her.

"Approach the bench," the judge said angrily. Once the lawyers were assembled, he continued, "You give me one good reason why I don't charge them and you with contempt."

"I had no foreknowledge of any of this, Ben," the attorney said. "They left word with my receptionist this morning and I only found out about it just before I arrived at the courthouse. I've tried calling and can't get an answer at the house or business."

"Then I'm issuing a bench warrant for both of them. Maybe a couple of nights in jail will teach them to respect this court. Step away."

When he was back at his table, the attorney said, "Your honor, I do want to formally apologize to Miss Messner for all of this."

"An apology isn't going to help your clients."

"The apology isn't from my clients, your honor. It's from me personally. I sincerely regret the pain they have caused her with this stunt."

Christine nodded to him and managed a weak smile.

"So noted," the judge said. "Christine Messner, please rise."

Christine stood with Elijah and gripped his hand.

"Since your parents have decided to defy this court, I see no reason to delay my ruling. Having found you to be a responsible and resourceful young woman and having been shown no just cause to the contrary, I hereby declare you to be emancipated under the laws of the State of Georgia, this day, 4 September 1989."

Christine was beaming. "Thank you, your honor."

"I wish you all the best, young lady," the judge said. "May you, at last, find the happiness you deserve. This court stands adjourned."

Back in Atlanta, the Standridges held a party at their home to celebrate Christine's victory. About halfway through the festivities, Christine stated she wanted to make an announcement and called Lawrence over.

"I've decided I'm going to change my name. Give myself a whole new start," Christine told those assembled.

"That sounds like a good idea, Christine," Lawrence said. "Might be just the thing for you."

She took Lawrence's hand, and addressed him and his parents. "Would y'all be terribly upset if I took the name Claire?"

"Claire?" Mrs. Standridge said. "That was—"

Christine nodded. "Yes ma'am." To Lawrence, she said, "I remember you telling me it was your sister's name. That you lost her when you were a kid. I know I can never replace her, but I'll do all

I can to live up to her memory."

Tears came to Lawrence's eyes and he hugged Christine.

Mr. Standridge put his arm around his wife and looked at her. She nodded.

"It would be a great honor to us for you to have that name Christine," he told her.

"What are you going to do for a last name?" Elijah asked.

"Haven't thought about that." Christine considered it. To Mrs. Standridge, she said, "What's your maiden name?"

"Belmonte," Mrs. Standridge said.

"Claire Belmonte," she said, then thought about it. "No. Claire Christine Belmonte. I kind of like how that sounds."

"You're going to keep your first name, then?" Lawrence said.

"We should always carry with us a reminder of where we came from," Christine said.

Lawrence embraced her. "I like that name very much — Claire."

Christine filed her petition for a name change before the end of September, and for supporting documentation, she used the ruling from her court case and affidavits from the sheriff's office about her treatment. Elijah, who had friends with the superior court in DeKalb County (which Christine now claimed as her county of residence) asked them to expedite the request.

So, it was, that on 10 October 1989, a few months before Zachariah and Selma Messner placed a headstone in the local cemetery for their daughter Christine, she was reborn in Atlanta as Claire Christine Belmonte. It was a couple of years before Claire learned of what the Messners had done, but every year afterward, she would travel to Houston County near the time of her birthday to lay flowers on Christine's grave.